D1235182

CURSED BY THE SEA GOD

Cursed by the Sea God

Odyssey of a Slave: Book II

Patrick Bowman

RONSDALE PRESS

CURSED BY THE SEA GOD
Copyright © 2013 Patrick Bowman

RONSDALE PRESS
3350 West 21st Avenue, Vancouver, B.C., Canada V6S 1G7
www.ronsdalepress.com

Typesetting: Julie Cochrane, in Minion 12 pt on 16
Cover Art & Design: Jake Collinge
Paper: Ancient Forest Friendly "Silva" (FSC)—100% post-consumer waste, totally chlorine-free and acid-free

Ronsdale Press wishes to thank the following for their support of its publishing program: the Canada Council for the Arts, the Government of Canada through the Canada Book Fund, the British Columbia Arts Council and the Province of British Columbia through the British Columbia Book Publishing Tax Credit program.

Library and Archives Canada Cataloguing in Publication

Bowman, Patrick, 1962–
   Cursed by the sea god / Patrick Bowman.

(Odyssey of a slave; 2)
ISBN 978-1-55380-186-3 (print)
ISBN 978-1-55380-187-0 (ebook) / ISBN 978-1-55380-188-7 (pdf)

   1. Trojan War—Juvenile fiction. 2. Odysseus (Greek mythology)—Juvenile fiction. I. Title. II. Series: Bowman, Patrick, 1962– . Odyssey of a slave ; 2.

PS8603.O97667C87 2013   jC813'.6   C2012-907714-3

At Ronsdale Press we are committed to protecting the environment. To this end we are working with Canopy (formerly Markets Initiative) and printers to phase out our use of paper produced from ancient forests. This book is one step towards that goal.

Printed in Canada by Marquis Printing, Quebec

for my wife Barbara,
who has kept us solvent while we've
kept each other sane

and for my daughters Kathleen and Anitra,
who still listen to all my stories

ACKNOWLEDGEMENTS

Although my name is on the cover of *Cursed by the Sea God*, there are many people I want to thank for their help: my family and friends, who endured long discussions of how to keep the plot fresh while remaining true to Homer's *Odyssey*; the students of the John Wanless Public School Book Club, who helped me identify the bits that went on too long or just made no sense; my indefatigable editor, Ron, whose patience knows no bounds; my sister Laurel, who provided invaluable insight into what was really motivating my characters; the wonderful folks of the OLA *Forest of Reading* program who chose *Torn from Troy* (to which *Cursed by the Sea God* is the sequel) as a Red Maple selection. And, of course, Ameera, for letting me use her name.

CONTENTS

CHAPTER ONE

The Windward Isle

SPRAWLED ON THE COBBLES, the girl was staring up, her dark eyes widened in horror. The slave's knot that bound her hair had shaken loose, leaving dark strands dangling across her face. But she wasn't looking at us.

For some reason she was looking up at a fruit seller, a greying man with gentle eyes. When the Greeks had emerged from the alleyway a moment ago, they must have startled her. A group of bronze-hard Greek soldiers could do that. Coming up behind them, I'd entered the square just in time to see her leap back in surprise. Struggling for balance, she had staggered into a rickety cart. It had toppled over, sending pears rolling across the cobbles and leaving her sprawled among them.

Now, a shocked silence had fallen across the busy square. "Please . . ." she began, her eyes pleading. I watched, wondering what she was so afraid of.

The fruit seller shook his head, his expression sorrowful. "I can't change the rules, young lady, no more can you." He reached down to help her up. "Perhaps . . . it won't be too bad."

A breeze stirred his hair and he stiffened. "Best to go now, then. You don't want anyone else blamed, do you?"

She bit her lip. With a last despairing look around her, she turned to trudge off toward the high castle on the far side of the square. People stared at their sandals as she passed.

Something was terribly wrong here. I'd felt it since we'd landed on the island that morning. Something about the way the townsfolk kept their heads and voices down, avoiding attention. Or perhaps it was the street vendors, holding their wares up in an eerie silence. Even the insistent breeze that had followed us up from the harbour seemed unnatural, snuffling beneath our tunics like a suspicious dog. And now, to my amazement, instead of running off with the spilled pears, the street urchins nearby were neatly piling them back on the fruit-seller's cart.

I bent to help. "So what's her problem?" I asked one of the boys, trying to sound casual as I nodded in the direction the girl had gone.

He looked sideways at me, the whites of his eyes showing

like a terrified horse. "Get away from here," he hissed. "Before you get us polished along with her." He put his pears in the cart and disappeared into the crowd.

We had sighted the island that morning, six days after our escape from the Cyclops. With our water cisterns empty, there'd been no choice about landing, and the sight of a sheltered harbour with proper wharves for mooring had made the decision easy.

The Greeks were led by a man they called Lopex. His real name was Odysseus, but nobody called him that. And for me, calling him Lopex also made it easier to forget that he was a Greek war leader. I could see him just ahead in the crowded marketplace, leading a delegation of five men to the castle on a hill in the centre of the city. I was pleased that he'd included me. Officially, I was just a slave, and a boy besides, but since I'd proven myself as a healer, and again while fighting the Cyclops, it was clear Lopex had begun to see me as something more. My chest puffed out a bit at the thought as I trailed behind the Greeks.

Up close, the castle was even larger than it had looked from the harbour, topped with a bronze tower pierced by four large, perfectly round holes open to the four winds. The girl had come this way only moments before, but there was no sign of her now.

"So, Alexi? Are you coming?" Lopex was waiting for me to follow, a wry expression on his face. I smiled as I realized he'd called me by name again and hastened to catch up. The other Greeks were already heading through the large doorway behind a servant who had come out as we approached. As I passed porters in the hall, I couldn't help wondering what their life was like. Their bare feet said they were slaves, but they still looked better fed than I'd been as a free orphan on the streets of Troy.

I twitched at the memory. I tried hard to avoid thinking of that life, but unguarded thoughts sometimes broke through. Troy, the city I had lived in all my life—until a few months ago. Until the Greeks got in.

After ten years of war, they'd somehow broken through the wall, killing everyone I knew and taking me as a slave before sailing for home. Soon afterwards, their own healer had been killed in a raid and they'd forced me, son of a Trojan healer, to take his place. That was probably what had kept me alive so far. And if they'd known I was really fifteen, they would have killed me before we'd even set sail. For once in my life, I'd been glad to be short for my age. If only my sister Melantha . . .

Those thoughts were even more painful. I'd felt sure I had seen her die that night, until my fellow-slave Kassander had said she was still alive. I just wished I could believe him. I forced my thoughts elsewhere by looking around the room we'd been brought into.

"Welcome, travellers." The voice was husky, with a slight lisp. I peered between the broad backs of the Greeks in front of me to see who was speaking.

"I bid you welcome to my land, the kingdom of Aeolia. I am Aeolus, the King." The king! I wormed forward to see a puffy-faced, shrunken man wrapped in a cloak much too big for him, sitting on an ornate raised chair. He lifted a frail hand in a languid half-wave. Nearby, a knot of brightly dressed courtiers clapped obediently. I peered at the king, puzzled. Surely he wasn't what everyone was afraid of.

The king gestured vaguely and the clapping trailed off. "Come over here, young man, and tell me who you are."

Lopex approached the foot of the throne. "My name, Your Majesty, is—"

"Majesty? Majesty?" A frown spread across the king's face like a cloud. "We don't use that title here. Call me 'Your Inclemency.'" He made that gesture again and the courtiers clapped once more, their elaborately styled hair bobbing like birds. "Now, go on."

"My name, Your—Inclemency—is Odysseus. Of Ithaca. Son of Laertes. I bring you gold and silver plate, ten fine bronze tripods, and able-bodied slaves as a guest gift."

The king just looked at him, the silence stretching so long I thought he'd fallen asleep. At last he spoke. "Son of Laertes, you say. A credit to your ancestors, you are." He paused again, nodding to himself. "Indeed, your ancestors." He sat up suddenly.

"Yes! Let us dine together. The men in your ships, summon them. They may dine—" He broke off, sniffing delicately in our direction. "They may dine in the old barracks."

Lopex bowed. "You are very generous, Your Inclemency. But you may not be aware that my ships hold over two hundred men."

The king's bushy eyebrows went up. "Aware? I assure you, dear boy, I know everything that passes on the ocean for five days' wind in any direction, including the strength of your company. It is no issue." He beckoned to an attractive slave girl nearby. "My dear, take our guest to the blue chamber. Bathe him well and dress him for dinner."

He tottered down the steps to take a seat on an ornate wooden litter nearby. Four husky slaves hoisted it to their shoulders as he waved gently to the room. The courtiers clapped once more as he was carried out.

That evening I ate at a small table in the corner of the kitchen with two palace slaves. Across the table was a heavyset boy about my age with dark hair, and on the bench beside me, a twitchy, anxious-looking boy a year or two younger. As the guest, I was invited to give my story first. By the time I had finished telling them about the Cyclops they were leaning toward me, round-eyed, to catch every word.

"After we escaped it, we sailed for six days before sighting land. We spotted your island at midmorning today." I dipped two fingers in a pot of their garlic *houmous* paste and smeared it on a piece of bread. "Now it's your turn. What's everyone so afraid of here? I saw a girl in the market square today, she was terrified. And your king—what's his problem?"

A look passed between the two of them. The nervous boy shook his head. "We . . . shouldn't talk about that," he mumbled, his eyes darting around anxiously. A momentary breeze from the hallway stirred his hair and he gave a violent twitch.

I frowned. "What's with you?"

The fattish boy shook his head. "You don't get it." He tried to lean across the table but couldn't reach. "Stelos, you tell him." The boy to my left leaned in reluctantly and cupped his hands around my ear. "The king listens," he whispered. "To the winds."

I tugged away to stare at him. "Listens to the winds? The wind from his own *gloutos*, maybe—" I broke off as the fattish boy leaned across the table and pressed a hand hard against my mouth.

"Don't," he hissed. "I'm not kidding." He stood up. "Stelos, let's get out of here."

I grabbed Stelos by the wrist as he got to his feet. "Wait!" I said. "What's going on?"

The noise was beginning to attract attention from the kitchen servants. The boy glanced around nervously as he tried to tug his wrist free, but I wouldn't let go. Finally he stopped. "Not here," he whispered, bending toward me. "Meet me tomorrow, after breakfast chores." I let him go and he almost ran out of the kitchen.

The next morning, I spotted Stelos carrying steaming plates out to the nobles' dining room. After the dishes were washed and the day's grain had been delivered to the slave girls for grinding, he nodded hesitantly in my direction. I followed him up two flights of stairs, more than I'd ever seen in a single building, to a storeroom filled with badly tarnished armour, and over to a window on the far side. From up here I could see the entire castle square. Yesterday it had been packed with people, but now it was completely empty.

Or almost so. In the dead centre of the square stood two bronze posts, each about a man's height, with a silver manacle on a chain hanging from the top. A stray dog lay between them, gnawing on a polished white bone.

I turned back to Stelos. "What are you showing me? Those whipping posts?"

He shook violently. "Not ... whipping," he whispered, looking down.

"Then what are they?" I asked. "What does this have to do with the girl from the market?"

There was a noise from outside, and I turned back to the window. Below us, two thickset eunuchs were leading someone out of the castle. As she looked fearfully at the sky, I recognized her as the girl from the marketplace.

The two eunuchs shackled her to the posts and retreated quickly into the castle. Stelos tugged my sleeve and pointed. "It's starting," he whispered.

I looked but could see only a tiny dust whirlwind scudding across the square. "What?"

Stelos led me to the far side of the room and plucked a

long thread from his tunic. "It's okay," he breathed, peering at the thread as it hung motionless between us. "They're distracted, for now."

I frowned. "Who? And what's going to happen to that girl?"

His eyes flickered to the thread, still motionless. "Listen to me, Greek." Irritated, I opened my mouth to point out that I was Trojan but shut it again. "The sooner you leave, the better," he went on. "They're everywhere. Listening. Even in the castle. Haven't you noticed, there are no doors or shutters here? Nothing to block the winds. *And they listen to him too.*"

This wasn't making any sense. "What's going to happen to that girl?" I asked, losing patience.

He shook his head. "There was a time when the king was fair, they say. Back when he was younger. But not now. The winds are worse now. No one even dares to get angry anymore. Step out of line and get . . . polished."

I grabbed his shoulders. "Polished? Someone else said that. What is it?"

"Those posts. That's where it happens." His voice faltered. "People get chained there. Then the winds come." He squeezed his eyes shut. "My own brother," he said, his voice breaking. "I saw him, after. The winds, they . . ." he broke off, burying his face in his hands. "Don't make me say it," he whispered. "But Ameera—they're coming for her."

"What?" I blurted. "Just for spilling those pears? That was an accident. We startled her! Can't we tell the king?"

He shrugged helplessly. "How? His court, they keep the

people from him. Now he hears only the winds." He glanced up. "Listen." From outside the castle came a low, whistling moan. "They're coming."

I shoved him aside impatiently and darted from the room to leap down the stairs. Speeding past huddled knots of courtiers and slaves in the hallway, I ran for the open front entrance and shot out into the square.

Ameera was standing between the two posts, her arms held above her head by the silver shackles. Whirlwinds of dust and sand flickered across the courtyard. Her hair was whipping back and forth in the rising wind.

"Ameera?" I called as I approached. She lifted her head in surprise. Her face was streaked with tears and dust.

"Who are you?" she said. "You're not from here. Get back inside!"

I stopped before her. "It wasn't your fault!" I said urgently. "We scared you yesterday. We need to tell the king."

She shook her head. "The king doesn't listen anymore. Not to people." She looked up and her face fell. "Sweet Demeter," she murmured. "It's too late."

A dark, swirling funnel was descending from the clouds like the finger of Zeus. "I don't understand," I shouted over the rising wind. "What will it do?"

"Don't you see?" she shouted back. "I'm to be *polished*." She looked around. "There." She nodded toward a white bone lying against the palace wall. "The wind does that. It picks up the sand, and . . . *polishes*. When it's done, there's nothing left.

Just bones." She squeezed her eyes tight. "Sweet Demeter," she called. "Please don't let it hurt, not too much. I've always saved my best offerings for you."

The chain rattled in the rising wind as I reached up to examine the manacles. The mechanism holding them closed was a simple clasp, but it took two hands to undo.

"What are you doing?" Ameera shouted over the wind as she saw me reach up.

"Getting you out of here! You didn't do anything! This is insane!" I shouted back.

"It's too late! Look!" she shouted, pointing up. I quailed as I saw the approaching finger of cloud, now nearly level with the tower atop the castle. The first manacle popped open as I twisted it and I moved to the second. The wind was shrieking now, tearing at my clothes. Sand whipped into my eyes, stinging my cheeks painfully. I closed my eyes and groped for the manacle by touch. The clasp was stuck, and as I worried at it with my fingers the roar from the wind took on an angry note, as if it realized it was being cheated. The clasp popped open and I pulled Ameera's slender wrist from it to haul her, stumbling against the wind's lash, across the courtyard and into the palace.

Somehow the wind knew it couldn't enter. We could hear it roaring in disappointed fury behind us. "It's no good," Ameera panted. "He'll just send me out there again. And this time you'll get it too."

"We have to tell him he's wrong," I said, tugging her along

the hallway toward the throne room. Astonished faces peeked out at us from doorless entranceways to either side as we rushed past.

The throne room had no doors, and I burst in with Ameera in tow. The king was sitting on his gold-inlaid chair against the opposite wall. Two lumbering servants moved to intercept us but we dodged around them.

"Most regrettable, I know, but order must be maintained," he was saying to Lopex, seated on a divan nearby. "Otherwise the people would do what they liked, and then where would we be?" He reached for a gold goblet on a side table, but stopped as he saw us standing there, surprise in his filmy blue eyes.

"What? What is it?" His face took on a slow frown. "You're the girl with the pears, aren't you? Why aren't you outside?"

He tilted his head for a moment, eyes closed, mumbling to himself. Opening his eyes again, he turned his head to look at me, his expression clouding over. "You did that? You freed her?" he asked.

I nodded. "Yes, Your Inclemency," I answered carefully. "But for a good reason. She—"

He held up a hand. "Tut, young man," he said. "Slaves answer only what was asked."

"But she didn't do it! It wasn't her fault!" I blurted.

The king tilted his head and closed his eyes again as though listening to a voice only he could hear. "Young girl of dark eye moved backward into market table," he murmured. "Pears spilled over ground, confusion, many stepped on. She stands before you now." He opened his eyes again. "I'm afraid, young man, you've made a mistake, and now I fear you must take a polishing with her." He leaned down from his throne and patted my shoulder. "It lasts only a short while," he said gently. "And then you may rejoin your friends. We bear no grudges here." He sat back with the air of someone who had cleared up a misunderstanding. The courtiers clapped.

I looked at him as he turned toward Lopex again. Rejoin my friends? What was he talking about? "NO!" I blurted.

The king turned back to me. "Young man," he said coldly, "I don't know where you come from, but in my kingdom, slaves speak *only* when spoken to. Now, you really must do as I say or it will be the worse for you." He turned back to Lopex. "Your slaves, are they all this troublesome?"

Lopex spoke from the divan. "I have found that when this boy speaks, his advice is often worth listening to, Your Inclemency. What did you want to say, Alexi?"

I hesitated, trying to understand. "Sire?" I asked. "Have you ever seen someone get—polished?"

"I? Of course not, boy. Not for many years." He tugged his cloak around his shoulders. "The winds were milder, and I was stronger. Now I am content to stay in the castle. My four winds, they tell me all I need to know."

An idea came to me. "Sire? May I have permission to leave for a moment? There is something I must show you." The king nodded absently. I grabbed Ameera's hand and we ran off for the exit.

Behind me, the king was remarking to Lopex, "Excitable,

isn't he, this slave of yours. What do you think he wants to show me?"

Ameera had the same question as we ran through the castle hallways. "Where are we going?" she panted.

"To the pillars!" I stopped at the front entranceway to peer up at the sky, but the dark clouds had disappeared, the swirling finger gone as if it had never been. "Bones!" I shouted as I ran out into the courtyard. "Grab whatever you can find!"

We darted around the square, snatching up the few polished bones that hadn't been carried off by dogs, and returned to the throne room. The king peered curiously at us from under his bushy eyebrows. "Young man, I must tell you that I am losing patience. Why are you bringing those into my throne room?"

"Please, Sire," I said. "Do you remember who you last sent to be polished?"

His eyebrows went up. "Of course. A king's duty is to remember. It was three half-months ago. A boy, younger than you. He kept talking back to his mother. We couldn't have that, could we?" The king shook his head as if in reply. "But his mother was soft. When I sent him for polishing, she began to scream. I should have had her polished along with him. Perhaps I am also too soft."

I dropped my armload of shining bones on the floor, and Ameera dropped hers beside mine. "I don't think so, Sire," I said quietly. "This is what was left of him, afterwards."

The king peered down at the pile of bones, blinking. "Bones?

Now why would that be?" He looked up at me. "Once again, young man, you are mistaken. Those are animal bones." He waved me away. "Mark him for extra polishing. He has wasted my time."

Two round-shouldered eunuchs appeared from somewhere and began to drag me toward the door, but Ameera darted in to pluck something from the pile. "Sire, look at this!" She held the bone out to him. "A jawbone. Not an animal's—a child's!" The king took it wordlessly, turning it over in his hands for some time before looking up, his expression puzzled.

"This bone," he said. "Where did you get it?"

"Outside. Near the pillars. They're always there, after . . . someone is polished." At his uncomprehending look, she went on. "The winds do it. With sand." She faltered. "This is all they leave."

He looked at her, then back to the small jawbone in his hand. Most of its tiny teeth were intact. The blood drained slowly from his face. He turned toward the courtiers, now huddled in an anxious knot.

"Did you know?" he whispered. They said nothing. He frowned. "You *knew*? Why did you not tell me?"

Someone gave an uncertain clap but stopped. A young man was pushed forward by the others. His hair was carefully sculpted and tinted to look like a bird of paradise. "Your Magnificent Inclemency," he murmured hesitantly, bowing low. "We . . . had no idea." As the king's brow creased, he added quickly, "That is, we had no idea that this was not your wish."

"My wish? *This*?" He looked up at Ameera. "How . . . how many of my people have had this?" He held up the jawbone.

Ameera shook her head. "Sire, I don't know. Ever since I can remember."

The king stared at her. "That long?" he breathed, his rheumy eyes clouding. "My people. They believe I could do *this*?"

The young courtier stepped forward, his ornate sandals clicking on the hard floor. "Sire?" he began, his voice sympathetic. "How terribly upsetting this must all be for you." He pressed his fist to his mouth, thinking. "I have it, Sire—a long, refreshing bath! That's what you need. The very thing for days like this." The courtiers behind him murmured approval.

The king had begun to get to his feet at the young man's words but stopped. His expression slowly shifted, grief giving way to a growing anger that creased his brow like a gathering storm.

"A bath, Thalpius? You think to wash this away with a *bath*?" The young man stepped back uncertainly.

"All of you," the king growled, sitting up on the throne, swelling and filling out his robes as though taking strength from his fury. "This!" he shouted suddenly, shaking the jawbone at them. "This is *your* doing! Too fearful to tell your king the truth. Afraid for your *status*."

He threw the jawbone to the floor where it shattered, sending teeth and bits of bone skittering across the tiles. "Get out," he hissed, his voice shaking with rage. "Leave my palace, or by the power granted me by Zeus, you shall feel the bite of the winds yourselves!" The huddled courtiers paused uncertainly, then darted for the doorway in a clatter of sandals.

He turned back to me, his eyes blazing. "And you, young man," he began, his fury out of control now. "How DARE you contradict the king? Do you know the punishment for that?"

He frowned at his words, staring at the shards of jawbone on the floor. "Contradict me. Indeed," he added, his voice softer. "There is not a soul among my people who would have dared." His blue eyes stared at me for several moments. "And yet you did. For that, it seems I must thank you." He gestured to the two eunuchs gripping my shoulders. "He may go."

As Ameera and I headed for the door, I heard Lopex speaking. "Your Inclemency, I truly regret that your winds have run wild. But if it is within your power, I believe I know a way to punish them and help me on my journey at the same time . . ."

CHAPTER TWO

There and Back Again

WHEN I WENT OUT to the market with the kitchen slaves the next morning, the stares and whispers made it clear that the story had gone around. The candy master, a short, plump man who made a sweet treat from boiled beets, insisted on handing me a lump of his sticky product whenever he saw me. Even the Greeks looked at me with a new respect. Life as a kind of underground hero on Aeolia was a pleasant change, and I began to feel a contentment I hadn't felt since before my father died.

It lasted for over a month, and then one day Lopex sent for me. I followed the messenger slave into a saffron-scented chamber in the palace. Lopex was seated on the edge of a richly padded divan, the king lying on a similar bench nearby. There were no courtiers in the room, but in a corner someone was strumming a harp. I looked again, startled. The harp was playing itself, a soft, smooth sound as though all the strings were being rubbed at once.

The king was speaking. ". . . like unruly children. Zephyros is a demon, of course, and never, never to be let loose. Notus of the south is my favourite; she is gentle, she is warm, her touch a caress against the cold slap of Boreas, or the angry scratch of Eurus from the East." He sat up as he caught sight of me. "You there! Boy! What are you doing here?"

Lopex answered. "I summoned him. He is my healer and message bearer. And his advice is sound, as you have seen."

The king nodded. "Very good. Carry on."

Lopex beckoned me over. "Alexi, I want you to go to the barracks east of the castle and tell the commanders of each ship that we are leaving. The king is providing water and provisions; they will be on the pier tomorrow. I want the provisions loaded and balanced, and the men ready to go by two hands past dawn, two mornings from today. Make sure the cisterns are completely topped—" he broke off as the king interrupted.

"And for you, Odysseus, I have thought hard about your suggestion. Come with me to the tower." Waving away the nearby slaves with their *basternion*, he walked out with Lopex, and I headed for the soldiers' quarters, my head spinning.

Healer. Message bearer. I caught my breath as a new title came to me. *Advisor.* He'd said so himself, hadn't he? My chest swelled at the thought as I strode into the barracks.

From the looks of the dining hall, the Greeks had done nothing but drink and fight for the last month. Along one wall were several round wooden containers, their lids pried off and dropped nearby. As I watched, a Greek soldier staggered up and dipped his goblet into a container near me. They were full of wine! No wonder I'd seen so little of the Greeks since we'd arrived. I was scanning the room for the ships' commanders when someone clutched at a fold of my tunic.

"Alexi?" I turned to see Pen, the young Greek soldier I'd saved after Ismaros, looking up at me with his dark calf's eyes. He was a little taller than I was but somehow always managed to look shorter.

"It's so good to see you," he added. "Were you looking for me?" He said something else but I didn't take it in, scanning the busy room for the Greek commanders. Eventually I realized he was waiting for an answer.

"Sorry, Pen. What was that?"

"I said, would you like to sit down and have some wine with me?"

"I wish I could," I answered, still searching the room. "Lopex has asked me to carry messages for him."

"I understand," he said, sounding downcast. "You're not just a healer anymore. I hear you're a hero now, too. You don't need to spend time with me."

"No!" I said, turning to look him in the eye. "That's not it at all, Pen. It's just that Lopex has me doing all these tasks. I'll try to come by later, okay? I promise." I caught sight of a knot of commanders sitting at a corner table. "I've got to go." Pen let his hand fall from my tunic as I turned to walk away.

"You!" I called out as I approached the table where the commanders were sitting. "Lopex wants the ships and men ready to sail by two hands past dawn in two mornings. Aeolus will send provisions and water to the docks tomorrow. You must load and balance them." My message delivered, I turned to go, but a hand yanked me back.

"So who are you to be telling us, slave?" It was Karphos, one of the fleet commanders, a tall man with an unkempt beard and bulging eyes.

I met his gaze confidently. "I am Lopex's message bearer and advisor." He glared at me and I felt emboldened to add, "But if you prefer, I can let Lopex know that you questioned his orders."

Karphos raised a hand to cuff me, but one of the other commanders caught his arm and muttered something to him. I caught the words *hagios*, the protected status that Lopex had granted me after the battle with the Cicones. Karphos let go of me reluctantly. "Don't get too big for your tunic, boy," he grunted. I turned to look around for Pen as I left, but he had disappeared.

The next day Lopex kept me busy carrying messages to supervise the loading. Ameera had cleaned my tunic and pressed it flat with heated stones, something I'd never seen before, and someone in the marketplace had offered to wash and style my hair. Nobody watching would have any idea that I was still a slave.

The Greeks were loading woven baskets of dried fish, beef and pork, along with amphoras of dates and wheels of cheese from the wharves. There were a few resentful glances in my direction, but nobody was about to risk Lopex's wrath by trying to make me help. I was watching the soldiers struggle to lower the heavy wooden water barrels into the hold of the *Pelagios* when I realized that they weren't filling the shipboard cisterns, but leaving the water in the wooden barrels.

"Hey!" I called. The men handling the water barrel looked up. "You need to store that water in the cisterns."

"Do we now?" one of them called. "So what makes you the expert?"

"Lopex's orders," I called back. The men didn't move, so I added, "Or do you want him to hear about it?"

The men shuffled their feet resentfully. "Somebody go fetch a bucket, then," one of them muttered. Ignoring their angry glares, I watched for a little longer before going off to tell the remaining ships the same thing, smiling to myself. I could get used to this.

At the bow of the *Pelagios* the following morning, watching the last of the ragged column of Greeks tramp down the street toward the harbour, I caught sight of Lopex, coming down the hill from the palace. Over his shoulder he carried a sailor's duffle bag made of thick sail cloth, cinched shut with a narrow silver cord. The sack looked fully laden, but as he came closer I could see it buffeting as if it held a flock of wild birds. Lopex had his big hands gripped tightly around the neck as though he didn't trust the cord.

The king had come with him down to the docks. In spite of his simple yellow robe, he seemed more regal now than he ever had with his clapping courtiers and *basternion*. As he gave Lopex a final hug, I overheard his warning. "Remember this: as long as the leash is tied, control will be yours. Let it slip, and may the gods show you mercy."

"Men! Ship oars! Raise the sail!" On board at last, Lopex was shouting orders from the stern, where, unusually, he had seated himself. The men stared at him, wondering. Even with my limited sailcraft, I could see that there wasn't a breath of wind to stretch the sail.

Lopex fingered the silver cord on the sack, a humourless smile flickering across his lips. "You want wind? I assure you, there will be. Now move! Procoros, signal the other ships to raise their sails and follow. Let the *Pelagios* take position behind the fleet." As Procoros turned to relay the orders, I stared at Lopex, wondering. The *Pelagios* always took the lead at sea.

After some manoeuvring, the ships were positioned with their sails up. The men looked around, puzzled, while Lopex bent to examine the sash on his sailcloth bag. He frowned as he noticed us watching him. "Turn around! Face forward!" he shouted. "You too, Alexi! Get below!"

As I clambered down the ladder into the bow hold, the

ship was buffeted by a powerful gust of wind, throwing me to the floor. Up top, I could hear the men cursing as they were thrown from their benches. "Eyes front! Stay at your benches!" Lopex roared. A moment later there was a second shudder, gentler. Suddenly the hull began to hum, as it did when we were running before what the sailors called a bride's wind. From the hold I could just see the sail, suddenly full-bellied. Where had the wind come from? I climbed partway up the ladder and risked a peek forward. Through gaps in the bow railing, I could see the other ships of the fleet ahead of us. Their sails were as full as ours.

Lopex's voice came to me clearly. "Eyes forward, men! In a few days, we'll be back home with our wives and sweet-hearts—and our wealth!"

Months ago, back when we were still speaking, Kassander had told me how Agamemnon, the Greek king who had started the war, had coaxed a magical wind to bring his fleet to Troy ten years ago. "He sacrificed his own daughter," Kassander had said, wiping his fingers on a tuft of beach grass by the slaves' dinner fire. "Cut her throat, then smeared her blood on the sail with his hands. It worked, though. After two months of a solid east wind, it shifted west the same day."

I glanced up at the sail with a shudder. Had Aeolus commanded his treacherous winds to follow us? And if he had, how was Lopex controlling them? If what I'd seen on the island was any sign, I wanted no part of it. But at least this sail had no blood on it.

We ran for three days before that eerie, constant gale. No gusts, no slackening, even at dusk when the day's breezes normally died. Filled by a perfect wind, the sail was so still that it could have been carved from a slice of marble, and the ship hissed across the smooth water like a knife. The men were ordered to sleep at their benches, facing forward and slumped against one another. Even when they relieved themselves over the side, they kept their eyes to the front. Only Lopex stayed awake through it all, glaring forward as though daring the wind to slacken.

He ordered me to keep my head down as well, but delivering food and water to the men at their benches gave me the chance to snatch glimpses of him at the stern. As far as I could tell, he wasn't doing anything special—just sitting at the steersman's seat, one hand protectively holding the string around his sailcloth bag, the other clutching at the steering oar. He never slept, and his stare grew more bloodshot as each day passed.

The men's spirits rose as the fleet crept nearer to home, the island of Ithaca. Even Lopex, now so sleepy that he could hardly keep his seat, seemed to brighten, while my own concern grew. I had earned a place here, but back in Lopex's household, would I be anything more than just another slave?

It turns out I was worrying about the wrong thing entirely.

The third morning after leaving Aeolia, one of the Greeks, a greying man whose skin had been tanned almost to leather, recognized the coastline of an island we were slipping past.

He spoke to the men seated near him, and soon an excited buzz of conversation filled the deck. One by one, other men began to recognize landmarks on nearby islands. We were almost there.

A noise from the sail made me look up. It was starting to flap, losing its taut shape. Ahead of us, the other ships of the fleet were slowing, their sails losing their curve as well. I risked a quick glance back at Lopex. He was slumped forward in his seat, his head across the neck of the bag, one arm still wrapped protectively around it. After three days and nights awake, he had fallen asleep.

I bench-hopped to the stern to wake him before the other men noticed, but his long stretch without sleep had left him exhausted. Even shaken, he didn't wake.

"Look!" came a shout from Ury, on his bench amidships. "The sail!" The men stared up at it. "Lopex!" he called. "The wind has stopped!"

Dead asleep, Lopex didn't reply. Ury loomed behind me. Grabbing my shoulder, he yanked me away and threw me to the deck.

"Well, well," he exclaimed. "Now we know why he didn't want us to look back." His voice was nearly a purr. "He's been holding out on us!" He wrenched the sack from Lopex's unconscious grip and began to fumble at the silver cord with his stubby fingers. "What's in here, anyway?" he muttered to himself. "Not weaponry or plate—too light. If you're wasting our time with spices, Lopex, I swear I'll stuff them up your *gloutos* and roast you on a spit!" The bag twitched beneath his arm as he tried to unpick the knot. Random gusts whipped at his face and tugged at the sail.

Suddenly I knew for sure what had to be in that sack. "Stop!" I shouted, scrambling up from the deck and launching myself at him. "That's not treasure!"

Ury glanced up and gave me a backhanded slap that knocked me against the stern railing. "Want some, do you?" His eyes narrowed. "Well, boy, why don't you come here and get it?" His free hand pulled a short knife from his belt. I circled, trying to approach, but the knife tracked me as I moved.

"Lopex!" I shouted. "Wake up!" The other Greeks had twisted on their benches to watch, but Lopex remained asleep. I feinted toward Ury, hoping to grab the bag, but his warrior's reflexes were too quick. Nearby, the port steering oar stood beside its empty seat and I ran to unlace it, hoping to use it as a weapon.

From behind me came a cry of triumph. I snapped my head around to see Ury sawing at the silver cord with his knife. Couldn't he guess what the sudden wind whipping his beard meant? As I lunged at him, the cord parted and the mouth of the sack billowed open.

A scream escaped the bag like a hurricane unleashed. Ury was blasted off his feet and thrown through the air into the sail, sliding down to sprawl across the benches below. In the sudden wind the ship bucked like a terrified steed, tossing first one, then a second screaming man over the rail to vanish into the churning sea below. I scrambled up the tilting deck, already slippery with salt spray, trying to reach the sack before it could empty itself. The ship was thrown the other way and pitched me headlong onto the sack. A powerful splash of salt water from the surging waves below broke across the rail, soaking me as I struggled to seal the sack again but without the cord, my hands were too weak to pull it shut.

"Alexi! What are you doing!" A shout came from behind me. I spun around, still grappling with the sack, to see Lopex, soaking wet from the last wave, struggling to his feet. He stared at the sack in my hands. "What are you doing?" he repeated. His eyes narrowed. "What have you done?"

"It wasn't me!" I bawled back over the howling wind, but he couldn't hear. Snatching the sack from me, he struggled to close it, but without the cord even his mighty grip couldn't force it shut, and the last of the wind whipped through his hands and out of the sack.

The ship began pitching wildly, huge waves coming at us from all sides at once. "Oars out!" Lopex called, dropping the sack and making an arms-out gesture. Tumbling back and forth on their seats, the men struggled to obey. "Phidios!" he shouted, beckoning the rowing master to the stern. "Zanthos and Praxy, take your places!"

As Phidios and the steersmen struggled back across the spray-slicked benches, I felt the motion of the ship change. The hurricane winds, until now dashing about randomly, had chosen a single direction.

Lopex identified it immediately. "Get that sail down!" he shouted. "The winds are heading home! Furl it now or they'll drag us with them!"

The men struggled, but the tension on the sail was too strong to undo the ropes that held it in place. Lopex growled and headed forward, knife in hand. As I struggled to keep my balance, another wave broke over the stern and knocked me over. The steady wind was piling the waves up into the same mountainous peaks that had nearly swamped us after Ismaros, bringing back Zanthos's words about the sail: *It keeps us ahead of the waves; without it, they'd spin us broadside and swamp us out!*

Struggling to reach the sail, Lopex hadn't noticed. The bow dropped as the *Pelagios* crested a wave and shot down into the following trough, leaving us momentarily out of the wind. Zanthos the steersman, wrestling with his steering oar in his seat nearby, saw the problem instantly. "Stop him, boy! We need that sail up!"

I stared at the pitching deck, the benches soaked with spray. Lopex had reached the port stay line, knife in hand. "It's too far!" I shouted over the noise.

"You've got a good arm, boy! Throw something!"

I glanced around and spotted the stern fire pot, long since extinguished by the waves. I staggered as I hefted it, trying to keep my balance on the pitching deck.

"Throw it! Throw it!" Zanthos was shouting. Struggling for balance, Lopex was sawing at the stay line as the ship climbed out of the trough. In a moment we would crest the next wave and the wind would catch us again. I took a breath and heaved the fire pot as hard as I could, aiming for his broad back. The weight behind the throw overbalanced me and I sprawled on the deck as the fire pot caught him squarely between the shoulders.

He staggered and spun about furiously but Zanthos took a hand from his oar to point at the waves. Lopex glanced angrily over the railing, then drew back, his face pale as he understood.

Only a day later, I watched him walk back down from the palace of Aeolus, his back hunched against a cold drizzle. It had taken us three days and nights to reach the waters of Ithaca, but swept before the full fury of that howling gale, we returned in a single day and night, bailing constantly to sweep out the water that cascaded over the bows. The winds had died as they returned to their roost in the bronze tower, and as we made the lines fast Lopex had walked up to the king's palace to ask the same favour once again. From his empty sack and slumping shoulders, the king's answer was clear.

I ran down the pier to explain but he threw the empty sack in my face. "This is your doing, you little *su'eromenoi!*" he said bitterly. "But for you, we would be home now. Was that your plan all along, *Trojan*? To keep me from my home and family?"

"It wasn't me!" I began, yanking the sack from my face. "Ury—" I choked as Ury came up and snapped his powerful left arm around my neck, cutting off my air and lifting me off the ground. I kicked frantically, trying to catch one of his shins with my heel, but I might as well have been kicking rock.

"I told you he was filth," he growled. "Didn't I tell you, Lopex?"

Unable to breathe, I struggled to pull his arm free. It was like trying to bend a bronze cart-axle. To my horror, Lopex nodded. "You were right, Ury. I should have known." He spoke up so that the ship's entire crew, clustered behind us on the pier, could hear. "I hereby withdraw this slave's *hagios*." He turned back to Ury. "Make it quick."

I twisted as best I could toward them. "Wait! Stop him!" I gasped.

Nobody moved. "Puffed-up little *koprophile*," someone muttered. "No more than he's got coming, if you ask me."

Ury draped me across the stone pier like a rag doll and straddled my chest. "I've wanted to do this since the day I met you, boy," he hissed, kneeling heavily atop me and clamping a hand over my mouth. I struggled to pull my arms free but he had pinned them painfully beneath his heavy knees.

"Go ahead, boy. Struggle. You and that sharp tongue of yours. I'll add it to my collection." His right hand, lumpy and misshapen with scars, stroked my ear as he buried his nose in my hair and breathed deeply. "Too bad we don't have a little more time."

Thrashing hard, I kicked my legs up to drive my knees into his back, but he just grunted and brought the knife up to my throat. Sweet Athene, was this it? Opening my mouth wide beneath his hand, I bit down hard, trying for a flap of his skin, but he snatched his hand away. He slapped it back over my mouth, but not before I had put my breath into a final, desperate shout. "Greeks! I'm your *healer*!"

It didn't work. Ury grunted in irritation and hooked his grimy thumb beneath my chin, forcing my head back against the pier and exposing my neck. I squirmed as I felt the knife-point. Even as I flailed, I felt my body tense, ready for the thrust.

"Hold, Ury." Lopex's expressionless voice came from behind me. "He's right. He's our only healer. You'll have to keep him alive until we get a new one. Until then he's yours. Just make sure he can still work. And you, slave," he added tonelessly, "If you ever speak to me again, I'll kill you."

CHAPTER THREE

Land of the Ship Breakers

"WATCH OUT, YOU sheep-hearted clod!" Yason, another scowling friend of Ury's, growled at me as I pitched into him on his rowing bench. Ury had tripped me as I came by with a water skin, sending me scrambling to keep from falling between the benches into the hold. I glared back, but Pharos, across from Yason on the same rowing bench, caught my shoulder and shook his head slightly.

He was right, of course. Since we'd left Aeolia for the second time, nobody would speak up for me, or even to me. Even Pen avoided my gaze, and Lopex acted as if I didn't exist. Pharos leaned toward me as he set me back on my feet. "Very bad, to be slave of Ury," he rumbled in my ear. "Young healer must take care."

No kidding. "On land, beware," he added quietly. "Be found never, outside of camp. Ury will not harm while Pharos is near." I glanced at him, surprised, but he had turned to face back out to sea again as though he hadn't spoken.

It was the morning of our fourth day out of Aeolia. The navigator had taken us north in search of the coastline but we had sighted no land, and now, after three hot days of steady rowing, the cisterns were running low. To everyone's relief, the navigator spotted a low cloud in the distance off the port bow.

We arrived at an island completely surrounded by high red cliffs that plunged into the sea. Circling it, we passed a tight inlet on the east side, and seeing nowhere better, Lopex had the ships turn and row back to it. By the time the *Pelagios* arrived, the other ships had already pulled into the small inlet through its narrow mouth, filling it completely and leaving us no space.

"Just as well," he muttered, watching their hulls grinding against one another. The navigator brought the ship right up against the cliff edge just outside the inlet, and we tied up to some straggly pine trees growing from the rocks.

"Ury!" Lopex shouted from the bow. "Take a couple of men and search the island. We need to know who lives here."

I ducked into the hold but Ury spotted me. "You! Thief!" he shouted down. "Get up here!"

Recalling Pharos's advice, I held my tongue. As I climbed back to the stern deck, a heavy coil of ox-hide rope landed on my shoulders, nearly knocking me back down the hold ladder.

Ury wrenched me up by my arm. I glanced around and spotted Pharos watching us from his bench. Ury, following my gaze, muttered something and let go. "Get up there," he grunted, pointing up the cliff face. "Tie that off at the top and drop the end down. And by the gods, if your knot doesn't hold, I'll throw you down the cliff myself."

I scrambled down the boarding net against the hull and jumped across the gap to the base of the cliff. There were no handholds in the rock, forcing me to pull myself up by grasping at the scrub pines that grew from the crevices, covering myself with their sticky, pitch-scented resin. Back in Troy, I'd never learned much about climbing, but I was small and light, and just here the cliff wasn't quite as steep. Even so, my hands were red and throbbing by the time I reached the top, my arms dotted with pinpricks from the needles.

"Move it, boy! Throw that rope down!" Ury's angry shout reached me clearly from the ship.

Scattered along the cliff edge were piles of irregular stones. I looped the rope around a large boulder nearby, knotted it with a surgeon's bind, then added three more for good measure and threw the rope down to uncoil as it fell.

From down on the stern deck, Ury's voice was just audible. "Get going, heretic." So he was sending Deklah first. I was suddenly glad I'd put in the extra knots. Deklah climbed onto the stern rail, tugged at the rope and scrambled up to join me at the top. Behind him came Yason, then Ury himself.

A steady, dry wind at the top whisked the sand across the flat plateau and into our eyes. Ury set off on a narrow trail that wound away between the windswept scrub brush and scattered boulders. The trail headed inland to meet up with a larger one, a gravel-lined road that took us down into a valley where the trees had grown into a patchy forest. A little distance inside it was a spring beside the road. A low rock wall had been mortared into place around it, creating a waist-high pool that was kept full by the spring inside.

"Huh." Ury scratched his head.

At that moment we spotted a barefoot woman carrying a small amphora on her shoulder, apparently to fill it at the spring. She was short and broad-shouldered, a vacant expression in her eyes. A flat nose covered half of her paste-white face.

"You! Slave girl! What land is this?" Ury called out, looking at her bare feet.

She lifted her head and faced around expressionlessly. Her flat gaze paused at us for an instant, but continued past us. As she reached the well, Ury tried again. "Do you understand me?" he said loudly. She raised her head and turned it in all directions, but once again didn't seem to notice us. Her amphora filled, she balanced it on one shoulder and turned to walk back the way she had come.

"What sort of imbeciles do they raise here?" Ury grunted,

striding forward to grab her shoulder, but Deklah caught his arm. "Wait, Ury. She's carrying that water back to town. We can follow her."

We fell into step behind her. If she heard our tread and Ury's occasional coarse comments, she didn't look back but proceeded down the road for a while into a small town, stepping carefully as though finding the path with her feet. At a second glance, it didn't look like anything I could have called a town. On either side of the wandering dirt road were dome-shaped huts of mud brick. Each had a single door, but no windows or chimney. As we followed the flat-faced girl up the winding road between them, we saw a few other trudging, thickset men and women with the same sightless gaze and broad nose as the girl. Most carried burdens on their heads or shoulders, wrapped in thick cloth bundles. Twice we had to dodge aside as a heavily laden man or woman trudged across our path.

"You know, there's something very strange here," Deklah remarked, apparently to nobody. "They don't even seem to notice us. You'd think strangers would get stares, at least. And they can't all be slaves, even if they are barefoot."

Was he speaking to me? I nodded carefully and tried a reply. "Nobody speaks, either." Even when two of them met, they touched one another's faces with their hands and parted without a word. Out of the corner of my eye, I could see Deklah's half-nod.

Just ahead, Ury fell back to walk between us. "What's wrong

with these people, anyway?" he growled, his eyes darting to either side. "They're acting like animals, or something." He caught my glance at Deklah and glared. "Do you know about this, boy? Speak up!"

I was opening my mouth to deny it when Deklah pointed. "Look there."

The road between the houses was coming up on a sprawling, low building of mud brick, laid in wandering courses. Dozens of seams in the exterior wall suggested it had been broken open and extended many times, and newer sections of lighter-coloured brick grew off it on both sides. The few irregular windows were small and high up, clearly for ventilation, not beauty.

Directly in the centre, two wide wooden doors were flanked by what had to be guards. Their eyes were as empty as all the others, but their faces were hard and hostile. Both wore identical dark leather breastplates and smooth, black helmets. Strapped across their chests were two cruel-looking curved scimitars whose sharp inside edges glittered with thorny spikes. Ahead of us, the girl walked right up to the wide wooden doors, which opened as she approached. The guards didn't move, and the girl vanished inside.

"Quick!" Ury hissed. "Follow her!" He sped up to close the gap.

"Ury, I'm not sure—" began Deklah, but it was too late. As the three of us reached the doors, the guards moved. Their scimitars flashed out simultaneously, the spiky inner edges digging painfully into the sides of our throats. Six more guards poured out through the double doors, seizing us and binding our arms painfully behind us. Yoked together by a twisted rope around our necks, we were yanked inside and hauled, stumbling on the dirt floors, through dim, downward-sloping tunnels. Pallid, hairless workers scuttled past, paying us no more attention than if we'd been bits of furniture. After passing several storerooms filled with giant earthenware pots, we were led down a ramp to a large, windowless chamber, the air inside uncomfortably warm and moist. As my eyes adjusted to the gloom, I gasped. Lying on her side atop a padded litter in the centre of the room was the largest woman I had ever seen.

In every sense, she was enormous. Standing, she would have been as tall as Pharos, but it wasn't her height that caught my eye. She was hugely, grossly fat. Her bloated arms were as thick as Ury's thighs, and her own pale thighs were so wide I doubted I could get my arms around one. Folds of fat surrounding her dark eyes had squeezed them nearly shut, and billows of blubber the size of two sheep wobbled beneath her coarse robe, threatening to ooze out across her padded litter.

Around her, a dozen hairless attendants fussed and twittered, cleaning her skin, brushing her hair and pouring wine between her lips from a wide-brimmed vessel. One stood by her head, chewing cake-like lumps from a bowl before spooning it out of her own mouth and into the open maw before her. I stared, horrified, but couldn't turn away. At that moment her expression changed to a frown of concentration, and a moment later, a foul smell crept through the moist air. From behind her vast buttocks another attendant appeared, carrying a broad silver bowl and poking anxiously at its steaming contents as she scurried off through one of the room's many doorways.

"Incredible," murmured Deklah, standing beside me. "That must be their queen. You know, I'd bet she'll spend her whole life on that litter." I didn't doubt it. There was no chance that mountain of flesh could stand up, even on those tree-trunk legs.

One of the attendants made a clicking noise, and the other workers stopped what they were doing to push and heave her bloated mass until they had rolled her onto her other side. I got a glimpse of her enormous buttocks beneath a leather girdle before the eight sweating men carrying her litter turned it to face us again and her attendants ringed her in once more.

Beside me, Ury chuckled. "Now that's what I call a woman," he muttered, his voice raw and earthy.

At the sound, the queen tilted her head to face us. Sausage lips twitched as she chattered a low-pitched string of chirps and clicks. The other attendants stopped what they were doing and looked up as her blank gaze swept across us, stopping at me. She spoke again and one of our guards severed the rope binding me to the other three Greeks with a precise twitch of one scimitar, then dragged me over to her. Another word from her and his blade sliced away the cord around my wrists.

This close, she was even more disturbing. The rolls of fat on her chin had merged into a single giant bullfrog sack that spread all the way down her breastbone, jiggling when she spoke. One corpulent arm reached out to slide field-mouse fingers slowly down my cheek. I stood stock still, desperately willing myself not to flinch. What did she see me as? A pet? A mate? A meal? I shut my eyes, sweat starting from my brow in the humid air.

In the silence I heard Ury chuckle faintly, licking his wet lips. "Looks like she likes you, boy," he called out. "Be sure to save some for the rest of us." Gods, I hoped he was joking.

The queen had turned her head at his voice and was chattering something. A guard with the other Greeks jerked hard on the rope around Ury's neck. He staggered, cursing.

"You want to jerk something, *gloutos*-breath?" he snarled, twisting around. "Jerk this!" Hands tied behind his back, he lowered his head and butted the guard savagely in the neck, knocking him backwards. As Ury's rush carried him forward, the rope binding him to the two others went taut and pulled them off balance. They tottered for a moment, then all three Greeks collapsed with a clatter, knocking two of the guards down with them.

The razor-sharp scimitars of the remaining guards flashed out instantly and landed on either side of the men's necks like giant pincers. One of them turned to face the queen and chittered a question.

Her frown could mean only one thing. I hesitated. I wouldn't cry if Ury died, but Deklah . . . besides, I wasn't likely to get out without them. I needed a distraction.

Before she could reply, I raised my hands to my face and

moaned loudly, bending over as though sick. As the queen turned to look, I hurled myself as hard as I could at the legs of the nearest litter-bearer.

Taken by surprise, he staggered, trying to keep his balance. A pale shin loomed in front of my face, and I grabbed it with both hands and bit hard. Pain shot through my jaw as my teeth struck bone. The litter-bearer screamed, bending to clutch his leg as I spat out a flap of bloody skin. Above me, the other bearers struggled to keep the litter level, but without their corner man, the queen's weight was slowly tipping it, dumping her huge carcass onto the packed dirt floor.

I rolled frantically out of the way as the queen landed almost on top of me, her mouth opening in an ear-cleaving shriek. The entire palace began humming like a plucked harp. Clucking attendants were suddenly running to her side from doorways all around. Soldiers rushed to form a ring around her, their swords waving in all directions like antennae, alert for threats. Workers spilled into the room, darting in to bundle her huge bulk back onto the litter, filling the entire room with their agitated clicks.

Keeping my belly to the ground, I crept past the soldiers to where the Greeks lay on the floor. The tiny corner of my mind that wasn't overwhelmed by fear wondered why the soldiers weren't coming after us, but I had no time to think about that now. Pulling Melantha's knife from inside my tunic, I sawed through the cords around Deklah's wrist and neck. Freed, he snatched the knife from me and cut Ury and Yason loose with a few quick slashes, tucking the knife away inside his own tunic.

As Ury began to scramble to his feet, his gaze darting around the room, I realized something.

"Don't move!" I whispered, grabbing his arm. "Look! They don't even see us!"

At that moment a clutch of workers poured through a nearby doorway and scuttled across us toward the queen, still squalling on the ground. Two of them stumbled over us on the floor but hardly slowed down.

Ury just stared at me, wild-eyed, but Deklah came to my aid. "You know, Ury, he's right! For some reason they aren't seeing us. Follow me and keep your head down. And don't attract attention!" He began to thread his way through the milling workers, crouching low. Ury hesitated, but I knew where my best chance lay. Springing to my feet, I ducked and followed Deklah toward the doorway, weaving through the crowded room.

I crept through the dim passageways behind Deklah, Ury and Yason now a few paces behind. Around us, workers and warriors were scurrying back and forth, chittering to one another. The hallways didn't look familiar, but I wasn't about to question Deklah's lead.

There was a soft grunt behind us and I turned to look. Yason, looking backward, had run straight into one of the black-carapaced palace soldiers emerging from a side room. One arm shot out and grabbed Yason by the shoulder. Ahead of us, Deklah turned, gesturing at him to stay still. Frowning slightly, the soldier stood facing him, cocking his head first to one side, then the other, staring with that strange, sightless gaze at what he had caught. As we watched, he drew Yason slowly to him and bent his head to sniff Yason's cheek.

Yason tensed nervously, ready to bolt. Deklah shook his head and gestured for him to stay still, but it was too late. As the soldier reached out for Yason's cheek with his free hand, Yason gave a frightened moan. Twisting out of the soldier's grip, he bolted up the passage toward us. The soldier spun, crossed scimitars emerging from their sheaths.

"Run!" Deklah shouted. We took off, the soldier pounding heavily behind us, scimitars waving in his hands. Close behind Deklah, I could hear Ury coming up behind me, and I risked a quick glance back. The soldier had nearly caught up to Yason. Clumsy with terror, Yason stumbled. Like a pouncing spider, the soldier was on him. With a single slash, he hacked a gaping slice from the back of Yason's calf. Yason screamed and fell to the ground, clutching his leg. In a swift, precise motion, the soldier swung both scimitars inwards like a giant pair of shears. They closed on either side of Yason's neck and snipped off his head.

Blood spurted in two jets from either side of the severed neck to spray the walls and floor as the head tumbled toward me. The sight left me frozen. The twin sprays of blood already dying to a trickle, the whitish stub of bone from the centre of the neck, and, worst of all, Yason's head, its unblinking white eyes staring from a shadowed corner, had pinned me where I was, horrified.

"Forget him!" I heard Ury shouting angrily. "Get going!" I turned, but he wasn't speaking to me. He was tugging at Deklah, his other hand gesturing at me. Yason was already forgotten.

With an angry glance at him, Deklah shook Ury's hand off and grabbed my shoulder. "Just run—they've noticed us!"

For a moment, I paused. Three more soldiers had emerged from a doorway, chittering with the one who had beheaded Yason, and began lumbering up the passage after us. We began running, and as we rounded the corner I glanced back for a moment. Workers with baskets and knives were already clustering around Yason's body.

Directly ahead were the double doors we had come in through, standing ajar. Putting on a burst of speed, we dashed through them into the open air of a cloudy mid-afternoon. Behind us, soldiers spilled out of the doorway into the square.

"Split up!" gasped Deklah, breathing hard. "Head for the ship! Warn them!"

Good idea. If those armoured soldiers caught one of us, there was nothing the rest of us could do anyway. I darted off the road and into the trees. If I could just keep my bearings, this route would be more direct, and I'd be harder to follow.

The underbrush was thicker than I'd expected. After working my way through it for a little while I paused to listen for pursuit. I could hear crashing behind me but it was a long way off, and I leaned against a tree trunk to catch my breath, waving away a cloud of sweat bugs.

Shortly after, I emerged from the forest near the top of a small ridge. Cresting it, I could see the scrub-strewn plain that we had crossed earlier, and beyond it, the cliff. The sounds behind me had died off. As I reached the cliff edge and turned to climb down the rope, a movement in the distance caught my eye. Coming over the ridge were Ury and Deklah. The shortcut I had taken through the woods hadn't been much faster after all, but it looked like they'd made it safely.

I looked again. Behind them, a black wave of soldiers was flowing up and onto the plateau, scimitars waving. Panicked, I half-fell down the rock face, giving my hands a painful burn on the rope. Seeing my haste, Lopex came back to the stern deck where I'd landed. "What is it, boy?" he barked.

"Yason's dead. Deklah and Ury—they're being chased by soldiers. They're almost at the cliff," I panted. This was not the time to stay silent, even if he had ordered me to.

He was instantly in command. "Lykos! Lykourgos!" he called to two brothers who sat across from one another. "Grab your sword and shield and get up that cliff. Ury and Deklah need your help." The two men snatched up their weapons from below their bench and went to scramble up the rope. They were only halfway up when Ury's wild-eyed face appeared at the top. "Get out of the way!" he shouted, waving them back as he started down himself. The two soldiers reversed course as Deklah appeared at the edge. I watched the rope strain under the weight of four heavy men.

Lopex saw the same thing. "Cut the bow rope!" he shouted to Procoros, pulling out his knife to do the same at the stern. "If they fall, better it be into the sea! Rowers to your benches; starboard side, unlace oars to push off!"

He was too late. As Lykos and Lykourgos jumped down the last few feet to the deck, I heard a snap from above and a wild cry. Arms flailing, Ury tumbled at least ten arm-lengths to land with a hollow thud on his back on the wooden deck. Broken rope still in his hands, Deklah dropped from the sky an instant later to land stomach-first on top of him.

I peered at them both as they lay motionless. A trickle of blood came from the side of Ury's mouth. Was he dead?

"Boy!" barked Lopex, unlacing an oar to push us off. "Look after them!" I rolled Deklah onto his back on the deck. Perhaps Ury would die before I got to him.

Had the soldiers reached the cliff top? I glanced up and gasped in shock. "Look out!" I yelled. "The cliff!"

Tumbling down the rock face at us were a dozen large boulders. Along the cliff, dark heads peered over the edge like beetles. "Row! Row!" Phidios shouted. The first boulders struck as the ship began to move. Three of them crashed into oars on the cliff side, snapping their handles out of their rowers' grip and momentarily fouling the others. Several others smashed down into the ship itself, lancing between the rowing benches into the hold, loudly smashing some clay *pithoi*. Another caught a forward rower on the arm. I noticed that, even with his arm broken, he had the sense to high-ship his oar to keep it clear, but the last boulder ploughed directly into the shoulder of Praxy, the silent port steersman, tearing his arm off and ripping him open from shoulder to waist. He slumped against his steering oar, instantly dead.

"Keep rowing, men!" roared Lopex from the bow. "They can't reach us once we're away from the cliffs!" He glanced upward. The cliff was still clustered with soldiers, but there were no more boulders coming down—yet.

The fouled oars had been cleared by their neighbouring oarsmen, and the *Pelagios* was pulling away from the cliff, about to cross the mouth of the inlet. The inlet! I'd forgotten about the other ships. Lopex was already in the bow, roaring at them. "Ships of Ithaca! Beware the cliff tops! Cut your anchor ropes and row out now!" No one hearing that voice could doubt its urgency, and the men of the other ships sprang to comply. They were packed so tightly that they jostled with one another to extricate themselves from the inlet.

"Sweet gods," one of the rowers muttered. "Look at the cliffs."

Around the entire inlet, the cliff tops had come alive with black, swarming figures. I bit my lip. Even Greeks deserved better than this. "Dear gods, get out, get out," the man near me was muttering, his knuckles white on his oar.

The nearest ship had managed to disentangle itself from the others by pushing off with its oars, and was now rowing furiously into the mouth of the inlet. I could see the captain, a youngish man with a light beard, holding the steering oar himself and scanning the cliffs to either side. Suddenly he froze, staring up. A mammoth red boulder bounced out from the cliff, crushing him instantly and tearing the entire stern from his ship.

Already low in the water, the ship sank quickly. Dozens of smaller boulders were smashing down in a deadly rain, destroying oars, crushing rowers on the ship and in the water alike.

"Sweet Hera," the man near me breathed. "It's blocked. May almighty Zeus protect them now." For a moment I didn't understand. Blocked? Then I saw. The mouth of the inlet was shallow, and the ship had come to rest on the bottom with its curved stern still visible above the surface. With that ship blocking the mouth, the others were trapped. A chill ran through me.

Lopex had spotted the same thing. "Swim for it!" he yelled. "Hold your breath and paddle with your arms. Dogs can do it, so can you!" Watching them floundering in the water, I realized with a shock that most of them didn't know how.

From deeper in the inlet came terrified shrieks and cries of pain. I wrenched my gaze up. Boulders of all sizes were hurtling down the cliff sides, bouncing off projections as they tumbled to spring out and strike anywhere in the inlet. With the ships packed so tightly, more boulders than not were striking ships, or Greeks.

"Get out of there!" shouted Lopex over the din. "Phidios, bring us in toward the mouth! Archers, up front! Fire at the cliff tops!" The ship began to move toward the inlet to bring the archers into range, but it was no use. The cliffs were too high, and long before we were in range, boulders began raining down on us again. It would take only one good strike to hole the *Pelagios* and sink us, and Lopex knew it. Angrily, he had Phidios back us off again.

He wasn't the sort to give up. I watched him carefully scanning the rock face on either side of the entrance, looking for a way up. I'd spent enough time with the Greeks by now to understand a little about tactics, and it was clear that the one way to save the men in the inlet would be a direct attack on the soldiers at the top. But the only climbable section of cliff was where we had moored originally, and the edge there still bristled with black figures.

In the inlet beyond the sunken ship, the pounding rain of boulders was battering the other ships to pieces. The water was crowded with the bodies of dead and dying men and the flotsam that had bobbed up from the holds. I watched in horror. Was there nothing we could do? Lopex had already deployed the boarding nets but none of the men in the water could get near us.

My eye fell on the jumble of ox-hide rope that had dropped back to the ship when it snapped, and a desperate idea came to me. Sweeping the bundle into my arms, I bench-hopped forward from the stern, pausing to ask Pharos to come with me from his seat amidships. He nodded silently as I explained, and bent to tie one end of the rope to a spare oar. I coiled the rope as I'd seen the sailors do and tied the other end off to the bow railing.

"Boy! What are you doing?" Lopex grabbed my shoulder. I turned nervously and explained.

He frowned. "Why did you not ask permission?"

I hesitated. "Well you said you didn't want to hear from me anymore."

He nodded slowly. "So I did." He wheeled on Pharos. "What are you standing about for? Do it!" Pharos hefted the oar like a harpoon, now anchored to the bow rail by a long rope. His aim wasn't good, but he could throw it twice as far as any man in the fleet. With a mighty one-armed heave he sent the oar arcing into the inlet to land well inside, the rope uncoiling from the deck as it flew. It speared the water like a diving seabird before bobbing back to the surface.

"Grab the rope!" shouted Lopex. "We'll pull you out!" I doubted anyone in the inlet could hear him over the mayhem, but words weren't needed. Already, several men were floundering toward it. A few who could swim were pulling companions along with them while others, clinging to drifting pieces of wood, were kicking their slow way past the sunken ship to safety.

"Pull!" shouted Lopex. Several other soldiers had grasped the idea and were hauling on the rope behind Pharos. Some twelve men were now gripping it and being towed toward the *Pelagios.*

The beetle-soldiers on the cliff tops had spotted the movement in the water and a renewed hail of boulders poured off the cliff, concentrating on the zone near the entrance. Within moments, five of the men on the rope had been struck, vanishing beneath the surface.

"Pull!" shouted Lopex again. Pulling so hard that the rope was in danger of breaking, they hauled the remaining seven men up to the bow. Lopex sprang over the railing to help those who were too weak up the boarding nets and onto the deck.

Pharos was pulling the oar out of the water for another cast, but Lopex touched his arm and shook his head. I looked up. The noise from the inlet had fallen away. The battered bodies of the Greeks and their slaves floated everywhere, motionless. There were no ships left afloat, no more heads above the water. From the cliffs, ropes were being thrown down, black-clad figures climbing down the walls.

Deklah staggered up behind me, holding one shoulder. In the panic I'd forgotten all about treating him. I wondered whether Ury was still alive. "What do you think they're doing?" I asked, watching the figures casting bronze grapples on ropes into the lagoon, reeling in the floating bodies.

He shook his head, rubbing the arm that had hit the deck when he landed. "You saw them. They were cutting Yason up and carrying him away in baskets."

CHAPTER FOUR

Circe the Sorceress

STUNNED AT THE LOSS of the rest of the fleet, the men sat at their benches on the *Pelagios* like corpses, too defeated even to shout defiance at the soldiers watching from the cliffs. Somehow, Lopex persuaded them to take up their oars again, while I was ordered to tend the few wounded laid out on the forward deck. Ury was still unconscious, which at least made him easier to treat. I used a couple of cooking skewers from the hold to splint what felt like a broken leg and left him where he was.

It was already late afternoon by the time we rowed away from the island of what we later came to call the ship breakers, and with no island in sight by nightfall we were forced to spend the night on the water again. We must have drifted during the night, because there was an island visible to the northwest the next morning. We pulled the *Pelagios* up on the first beach we found, a narrow gravel strip on the northeast face of the island, strewn with driftwood and uprooted seaweed from a recent storm.

For the next two days the Greeks lay groaning on the beach, their heads wrapped in rags. Kassander said it was a Greek thing. Fortunately, I didn't see much of Ury. He was awake now and sitting up on deck, but with his broken leg he couldn't climb down the ladder to the beach. He was also coughing blood, so there must have been something wrong inside, but it was nothing I could fix, even if I'd wanted to. I was assigned to bring the men water where they lay, but none of them ate.

On the third morning, Lopex got up and headed inland. He came back to camp mid-afternoon, carrying the carcass of a stag over his shoulders and leaning on his spear. After two days, I thought the men would jump up at the sight, but they didn't move. Lopex went a little way upwind, built a driftwood fire, then skinned and cut up the stag and started cooking it on skewers.

After ship's rations, the fresh venison smelled incredible. Lopex waved me over. "Boy! Over here!" He thrust a handful of skewers wrapped in an empty millet sack at me. "Eat."

Eat before the Greeks? A quick way to get beaten senseless. But the meat smelled too good to think about it for long. I pulled a piece off one of the skewers and bit in. "Stop," Lopex added, gesturing down the beach with his knife. "Stand over there."

Fine by me. I wasn't keen to be around him either. I walked over to where the men lay on the beach and continued eating. Nearby, Lykos rolled over and sniffed. "What's that, boy?" He peered at it. "Fresh meat? What are you doing eating before free men, slave boy?" Several other Greeks were sniffing the air and looking in my direction.

I shrugged. "Lopex gave them to me." I clutched the skewers tightly and suddenly understood. The men were too depressed to eat if he ordered them, but let a slave eat before them? Half a dozen Greeks were suddenly clustering around me, anger in their faces. Once again, I was only a finger's width from a beating. I held the skewers out reluctantly, adding ". . . to, um, give them to you."

The nearest men snatched them from me as the others, looking disappointed, headed toward the cooking fire. I watched them go, seething. Once again, Lopex had used me, and I hated him more than ever for it.

Sitting alone in the shade of a stubby palm tree on a hill behind the beach, I was still angry a little later when I spotted someone approaching. It was Pen. He recoiled as he caught my expression, but hesitantly held out a venison skewer. "Hi, Alexi. Would you like this? I thought you might be hungry."

I grunted something and took it. Pen glanced around before sitting down to watch me in silence. After a moment, he spoke. "Alexi?" He began, awkwardly. "I wish you . . ." He gulped and tried again. "I'm sorry. About, well, you know. Being given to Ury. And how he—"

"Nearly killed me," I interrupted. "I was there."

Pen looked like he was about to cry. "I'm so sorry, Alexi. I wish I could have done something to stop him, back on the docks. But nobody listens to me." He brightened a little. "But they did listen to you, didn't they? Lopex stopped him."

He was right. They wouldn't listen to Pen if he called them to supper. "Don't worry about it," I said. "It's not your fault." I finished the skewer and handed it back to him. "You'd better head back. It won't help if they see you talking to a slave."

The next morning, Lopex called a council on the beach. Clearly recovering, Ury roused himself to hobble down the ladder, along with one of the men we'd rescued, a man named Phaeton whose foot had been crushed by a boulder.

"Men of Ithaca!" Lopex said. "We have suffered a terrible loss. While you grieve for the men you knew, I grieve for every life lost from our company. As their leader, their lives were mine to command, yet I would never have chosen a death like that for such brave men. We are alive, thanks be to the gods, and with their blessing will remain so. We owe it to the memory of our shipmates to take up again the lives the gods have given us."

"Lives?" Deklah broke in. "How can we do that? Do you know how to get home? How to bring our dead fleet mates back? You talk about plans, Lopex, but look around. The gods haven't given us *kopros*. They want us dead."

I waited for Lopex to lash back, but he shook his head patiently. "Deklah. If the gods had wanted us dead, they could have caused it twice over by now. You, who went deep into the den of the ship breakers and escaped alive, don't believe the gods are on your side? For shame."

He raised his voice. "Before we continue our journey, we must hold a sacred feast to send the shades of our comrades to Hades. But our stores are low, and we have neither the equipment nor the time to replenish them. We must seek out those who live on this island and trade with them for food stores."

I felt a chill. Our encounters in the islands so far had all turned out badly. The men clearly felt the same way but Lopex cut them off, ordering them to split into two groups. The men shuffled apart obediently, the six or seven black-haired, scowling figures who I now thought of as Ury's crew all clustered near him. I circled around carefully to the far side of the other group.

Lopex spoke up. "Listen now. You men will come with me." He gestured at my group. "We will find the source of some smoke I saw yesterday; the rest of you will stay with the ship as a reserve, under Ury. Twenty-two well-armed warriors can stand their ground against whatever they find, or beat a safe retreat if they cannot."

Lopex stood up to put on his armour when Deklah spoke up again. "So why does it have to be us? Why can't it be Ury's group?"

Lopex closed his eyes for a moment, breathing carefully,

then opened them again and removed his helmet. "Very well, Deklah. You may choose who goes. Here is a wooden skewer. One end is burnt; the other is not." He snapped it in half and put both pieces in his helmet. "If Deklah draws the burnt piece, my group will go. Otherwise, it falls to Ury's group."

He held the helmet over his head while Deklah reached into it. The men fell silent. A murmur ran over both groups as he opened his hand to reveal the unburnt piece.

Ury glared at Deklah and struggled to his feet, leaning on a crutch made from a broken oar. "That's it, men. The heretic has stuck it to us. Now get your armour on and get moving!" He caught sight of me before I could dodge behind someone. "You, boy!" he snapped at me. "Get over here and help me with this armour!" As his slave I had no choice, and I cursed to myself as I joined them. At least this group had Pharos in it too.

We set out, Ury gripping my shoulder with one black-haired paw and leaning on his makeshift crutch with the other. Hiking up into the hills behind the beach, we headed for the interior of the island where Lopex had seen smoke. It was a hazy day with no breeze, so we were soon surrounded by clouds of sweat bugs. Ury cursed me roundly as we walked, variously ordering me to slow down or speed up, but with both hands occupied he couldn't cuff me. As our path continued uphill, the vegetation changed from low scrub to a thin laurel forest, leaving Ury muttering angrily about Deklah each time he had to hobble over a fallen tree.

As we emerged into a clearing, the men in the lead stopped.

"What is it? Keep going!" Ury called. Shoving me aside, he crutched his way up to the front to see what they were staring at. I followed, staying behind the soldiers, but stopped. In the clearing dead ahead, a huge cat lay in the shade of an oak tree. I peered at it. No, not a cat. A lion.

It looked in our direction, its tail twitching, and climbed slowly to its feet. I watched Ury struggle to back up with his crutch. "Don't run," whispered someone. "They're like cats. They like to chase."

I couldn't have run if I'd wanted to. Even from behind armed warriors, the sight of that huge beast padding slowly toward us was terrifying. The men groped for their swords. I'd never seen a lion, but this didn't look like an attack. It was walking casually toward us, like a man coming to investigate a beetle in his garden. As it reached a patch of sunlight in front of us, it stopped, then lay on its back and stretched its furry belly in the sun.

"What's it doing?" Ury hissed. The creature stretched again, then turned its head to face us. A low growl escaped from it as its front paws batted the air.

"I don't believe it. I think it wants a belly rub!" blurted the soldier who'd spoken before. He glanced around at us, looking embarrassed. "I once knew an Egyptian trader who kept a cat," he said awkwardly. "This is a lot like it, but bigger."

A lot bigger, I was guessing. The beast growled again, louder. The soldier must have been sure of what he said, though, because he edged up slowly and reached out carefully to touch its furry stomach. A rumble like a distant earthquake emerged from its belly. Slowly, the other Greeks approached, clutching their swords. Ury stayed well back.

A second lion lay contentedly in the clearing, but it stayed where it was as we crossed. On the far side stood a high stone wall with a bronze gate set into it. It wouldn't stop those lions, but they seemed tame enough. Or at least well-fed. The Greeks flattened themselves against the wall on either side of the gate. A soldier named Polites, who had somehow kept his tunic clean and beard trimmed through all our hardships, crept up and peeked inside.

"There's a stone cottage," he whispered over his shoulder, "with a garden. There's a spinning wheel and a few chickens. Wait, there's something coming. It's a woman. Now she's sitting at the spinning wheel."

"Does she look dangerous?" whispered Ury hoarsely, leaning backwards on his crutch. "We should head back. She keeps lions . . ."

Polites shook his head. "No weapons. I think we should be able to handle her."

Ury glared around at the others but got no support. "Get on with it, then," he grumbled.

Polites cleared his throat and called out. "Hello?"

After a moment the gate opened and a tall, fine-featured woman with high cheekbones and a nest of curly hair appeared. "I wondered when you would work up your nerve to call, good sir," she said, her voice a high-pitched chirp. "I am named Circe," she added.

Her hand flew to her mouth as she came out and saw the rest of us around the corner. "Oh! I didn't realize there were so many of you." She hesitated. "Well, I suppose . . . I suppose you should all come in. Yes," she added, her head bobbing, "that's it. Of course. Do come in, my lords. Please."

At her request, the men dropped their armour and weapons at the gate. Circe showed us across the flagstones and into a sunny room scattered with wooden stools and small tables. Colourful woven tapestries covered every hand-span of the walls. I trailed behind the men and took a seat in the corner, wondering why Ury wasn't ordering me over. Come to think of it, where *was* he?

Circe's voice distracted me. "Please, sit down, do," she said, her long-fingered hands fluttering like tethered sparrows toward the stools. "You've come from far away, I can see that. You must be thirsty in this heat, my lords. Thirsty, yes," she repeated to herself. "Perhaps you would like some wine, perhaps, some cool wine?"

I hadn't realized just how parched I was, but the idea suddenly seemed wonderful. The Greeks agreed enthusiastically, and she went into a back room, returning a moment later with goblets and a beautifully decorated deep bowl that the Greeks called a *krater*, from which she dipped wine for us all.

It was a light Pramnian wine, sweetened with honey and a sprinkle of white barley meal, but after only a single cup I felt myself growing strangely thick-headed. Around me, the conversation was slowly drying up, the Greeks slumping motionless on their stools. My thoughts were becoming slow and stupid. A goblet dropped from someone's fingers and clattered against the stone floor. For some reason it didn't seem worth turning my head to see.

I could hear Circe enter the room to my right. She walked past me and picked her way delicately through the seated men, pausing in front of Polites. "I'll start with you, I think." Her tone was sweet and high-pitched. "You naughty man, you didn't think to tell me there were others, did you? But then, that's just like a man, isn't it?"

She was carrying a delicate brush in one hand and a tiny glass amphora in the other. I watched, unblinking, as she dipped the brush by its golden handle into the amphora. The bristles glistened as though coated in oil. She turned to Polites and brushed his ears and nose with it, then put the amphora and brush down to watch.

Even in my stupor I was alarmed. His ears were growing! As I watched, they grew hairier, thinner, and developed points on the ends. His nose stretched up and back so I could see his nostrils, then flattened itself on the end. Like a—

Circe clapped her hands and squealed. "Oh, I do so love pigs!" She spun around, her long skirt flying out around her. Behind her, the transformation was quickening. Polites' head had become a pig's, his body was shrinking and becoming rounder, his legs and arms shrivelling, his feet and hands twisting and hardening into trotters. With a frightened squeal, he slipped off the bench and began to run around, snuffling at the floor and grunting wildly.

She turned to Pharos, seated motionless on the next stool, and stepped over his long legs stretched out before him. "Your turn, my pet. Aren't you a big one! But don't be scared. It's all for the best. You must trust me, you know." She leaned closer and pouted. "No? Well, you'll understand very soon." She brushed his nose and ears with oil as she had before. In a few moments, there was a second pig, much larger than the first, grunting on the floor by her feet.

Despite the fog over my thoughts, I felt a growing horror as she worked her way across the room, struggling to shake off my paralysis as she stopped before me. She made a pretty frown for a moment, one slender fist pressed to her lips. "You're a tiny one, aren't you?" she chirped. "You're going to make such a cute pig, I just know you are. I think I'll have to keep you for a house pet!" I saw the brush coming toward my face and made a last herculean effort to stop her but my arms wouldn't even twitch.

For an instant I thought it hadn't worked, but all of a sudden my balance was . . . wrong. I toppled from the stool and landed sprawling on my stomach. I tried to scramble up but somehow my arms weren't long enough anymore. Something large and pink was blocking most of my vision, and for some reason I could suddenly see nearly all around me. I opened my mouth to shout but all that came out were grunts and squeals. The fog lifted from my mind and I understood: I was a farmyard pig! Farmyard? The word stopped me in my tracks. Gods. Was she raising us for food?

There was a sudden smack on my backside as Circe swept us out the back door with a broom. "Out, out, no pigs in the house, you know!" She paused and looked at me. "Well, maybe just one, you cute little thing. But not until you're house-broken, of course," she added hastily.

She bent down to pick me up and I squealed angrily as she rubbed my neck. "Oh, just look at that curly little tail!" she exclaimed, tugging on something behind me. "You just don't know how cute you are. No you don't!" She lifted me to rub her nose in my face before putting me down again.

"There now, my pigglies. Don't you all feel better? I just want to help you, really I do. And don't worry that you can still think like men. In a few days, that will wear off, and you can get on with being real pigs." She leaned on her broom, her eyes shining. "Just think of it—rooting for beech nuts, climbing trees . . ." She paused, floundering. "Or, um, what-ever little pigglies like to do in the forest. But you'll be happy, you'll see. I promise!"

Her words set off a frantic squealing and grunting from us all. Surely there had to be some way to make her turn us back. But she just smiled and waved a hand at us. "Oh, please, don't. There's no need to thank me. I did it because I wanted to!"

She turned to collect some handfuls of acorns and beech nuts from a large amphora by the back door. Throwing them down to us, she added, "Oh, such an important thing, and I nearly forgot. You really must watch out for the other animals. Pigs are awfully tasty, and I'm afraid that some of the other men I've set free have very, very sharp teeth and big claws now. But don't worry, you'll know them when you see them."

She glanced up at the sun. "My goodness, look at how late it is, and I haven't even started my housecleaning yet. What must you think of me? Well, enjoy yourselves, and stay well, little pigglies. I'll be back out to feed you tomorrow!"

CHAPTER FIVE

The Conquest of Odysseus

THAT NIGHT BEHIND the sorceress's cottage was the longest in my life, worse even than the night in the Cyclops' cave. We huddled in a corner of the narrow yard, terrified that one of those huge lions would sniff us out. A stone wall wouldn't even slow down creatures like that, I was sure. And if the lions didn't get us, we would lose our minds and become thoughtless pigs in a few days, most likely to be slaughtered and eaten.

At least I wouldn't go alone. Speaking of that, what had happened to Ury? I couldn't remember seeing him since we'd come through the gate.

The sky gradually brightened as dawn approached. Morning came, and Circe appeared at the door to toss some more nuts to us. I'd never eaten acorns as a human, but they were strangely tasty now. "Feeling better yet?" Circe trilled. "Don't worry, you will soon, I know!" The door banged shut.

Some of the Greeks, especially those such as Pharos who had become larger pigs, were spending their time trotting up and down the walls of the enclosure, looking for a way out. I couldn't imagine why; that's where the lions were. Smaller than the others, I huddled alone by the back door, hoping they wouldn't trample me with their sharp trotters. As a result, I was the only one who heard what happened next.

For a while, all I could hear was Circe singing something tuneless as she went about her chores. The spinning wheel clicked from the garden out front, then stopped. I could hear voices but couldn't quite make them out. Eventually, they came inside the cottage and I could hear them more clearly.

"Would you—would you care for some wine, my lord?" Circe sounded breathless.

"No," came the flat reply. "I'm looking for my men. They came this way yesterday."

Lopex! He could free us! But his next words chilled me. "Just a little, then, while we talk."

I could hear her drawing a dipper from the amphora and pouring it into a goblet. A stool scraped as though it was being pulled up. "Now, tell me about yourself," I heard her say. "What brings a handsome man like you to my little cottage?"

Another stool scraped, and I heard Lopex approaching.

His face appeared at the open window. I could hardly look high enough to see him. The gods had clearly designed pigs to watch the ground, not the skies. Holding the goblet before his lips, he tipped it carefully the other way, pouring its contents out the window. "A fine yard of pigs you have here, Circe," he remarked loudly as the red wine spattered in the garden beside me.

Tilting the empty goblet against his lips as if draining it, he turned back to face into the room. "As fine as this wine you've served me." He wiped an arm across dry lips. "But I must ask you again whether you have seen my men." It was strange, as a pig I could hear every word as clearly as if I was standing between them.

Circe's voice sounded uncertain. "Your men? What, um, men were those? Oh! Of course. *Those* men!" She laughed, a nervous, high-pitched twitter. "Oh, yes, they came. I served them some wine, and then they left. They said they were going hunting. That was it, going hunting."

Lopex's reply was low and mumbled. For a little while the only sound was his breathing. Then there came the sound of a goblet crashing to the floor and I heard Circe push back her stool.

"Hmm." I heard her murmur as she got to her feet. "What sort of creature are you? Never a pig, not you, my sweet, no. A noble, forceful man like you?" She clapped her hands. "Of course! A man like you must be a wolf!"

I heard her footsteps disappear into her bed chamber and

return a moment later. "You're going to like being a wolf, my sweet. A lone, lean, cunning wolf. Now . . . just hold steady, that's right."

Suddenly there was a frightened squeal, and Lopex's flat voice. "Put it down. Now." Then the sound of a tiny jar being set hastily on a table. "Now tell me what really happened to my men."

Circe sounded as if she was having trouble speaking, most likely because of a knife at her throat. "Who . . . who are you? How did you resist my potion? Please let me go. I won't hurt you!"

"Swear it, witch!"

I heard her squeak in pain. "Please, I—" There were sounds of someone struggling to get free. "All right. I swear!"

"The strongest oath you know, witch!"

"Please, stop! You're hurting me!" Her voice was still strangled. "I swear . . . I swear on the mighty river Styx itself that neither I nor my creatures will harm you or your men from this point on."

There was the sound of a knife being re-sheathed. A moment later her voice came again, no longer choked. "But how did you resist my charm?" Her voice went soft and sultry. "Such a muscular man, too."

His voice grew deeper. "Resist your charm? Perhaps . . . not entirely." Then their voices went off into another room and I couldn't hear them any longer.

It seemed a long time before I heard anything further from

the cottage. At last there were footsteps approaching the back door. I trotted out of the way as it opened and Lopex stepped out, Circe hanging on his arm. Her feet were bare, her toenails painted an eggshell blue. His sandals had been mis-laced.

"So, Circe. Where are my men?"

She turned her gaze up at him. "Are you sure we have to do this right now? Perhaps later, after we've had dinner, or . . ."

He frowned impatiently. "Now."

She pouted. "Oh, very well. But you have to understand that it was for their own good. Most men are nearly pigs already, you know. Not you, of course, my lone wolf." She reached up to stroke his ear but he shook her off.

"For the last time: *Where are they*?" His expression changed slowly as he looked down at us milling anxiously at his feet. He turned to her, his expression shocked. "Pigs? Are *these* my men?"

Startled by his sudden anger, she said nothing. He grabbed her forearms and shook her savagely. "Speak, witch! Did you turn my men into *pigs*?"

She cringed. "Oh please, stop! It really was for their own good, don't you see? I just *know* they'll be happier, once they get used to it . . ."

"Their own good? *Pigs*?" he roared. "Turn them back at once!"

Her hands fluttered nervously. "Yes, yes, certainly. Anything for you, of course. But please don't shout, my sweet—it scares me."

He lowered his voice. "Turn them back now." He stooped to snatch up one of the nearest, gripping it in both arms as it struggled. "This one first."

"Yes, my dear," she said meekly. "Now, let me see." She frowned, concentrating, then brushed its nose and ears with her hand and murmured something. The pig immediately began to grow and change shape, and Lopex put it down hastily. In a moment the pig was gone and a white-haired soldier called Adelphos was crouching on all fours in the dirt before them, naked buttocks high in the air.

Circe took an involuntary step back. "Oh. Why . . . yes," she said faintly, a blush creeping up her neck. "Yes. Of course. Do you know, I've never actually changed one back before? Let me see about some clothes."

Adelphos stood up easily before her and she reached out to brush both his shoulders with her fingertips, her mouth pursed. "There." Now he stood before them in a simple *chiton* and leather sandals. "Your, um, armour is in the back store-room. Through there, yes, that way." She flapped her hand toward a door.

Lopex led her around the yard, transforming us one by one. Once again, I didn't feel the transition, but suddenly I was standing naked, my bare feet and hands in the muck of the yard, while she furnished me with clothes, including a pair of sandals like those she gave Adelphos. As a slave I wasn't supposed to have them, but Lopex had given me some when he had made me healer, and Ury hadn't thought to revoke them.

"That's it, men. Let's go," Lopex barked in his usual fashion, waving us toward the door.

"Go?" she repeated, trailing behind him into the cottage. "Already? But . . . I thought perhaps . . ."

"Not possible." He shook his head, sounding gruff. "I'm responsible for these men. I must chart our route home, find provisions for them, ensure the wounded—"

"Provisions?" she broke in eagerly. "Oh, but I can help you with all that! I do have powers, you know. And your course, I can help you chart a course home. I can even tell you of dangers, the dangers you will meet on the way."

Lopex paused. "I can feed all your men, too," she added. "Do stay, my sweet. At least for a little while. Tonight I'll prepare a special banquet for you. And your men, of course." Clasping his arm, she leaned in toward his ear and whispered something.

Lopex shrugged. "Very well. We will stay. Now I must return to my ship to fetch the rest of my men." He pointed to me. "You, boy. Come."

He said nothing as we walked back through the forest, but as we approached the beach where the ship lay, he spoke.

"Boy."

"Yes, sir?" It took all of my effort to keep the anger from my voice.

"What happened to Ury at the cottage of the witch?"

Surprised, I fumbled with the question for a moment. "The cottage?"

"Yes, boy, the cottage! What did he do when you arrived?"

Oh. "Uh, I don't know. I never saw him after we went in."

Lopex didn't answer. As we emerged onto the beach, he gestured at me to stay out of sight while he went on. When we had arrived, the men had been too despondent to draw the ship out of the water, and it was still resting half in the shallows. I hid behind the hull, watching the armourer hammer a hot bronze patch onto a badly dented breastplate nearby.

"I told you there was nothing you could do." Ury's sulky voice came from somewhere close. "Now let's get going, before those animals of hers sniff us out."

"Are you so sure, Ury? Perhaps some of your men escaped. We owe it to them to wait." Lopex's voice had a dangerous rumble.

"Wait?" Ury burst out angrily. "Did you see those lions? And those aren't the only ones, I'm sure of it." I heard him take a deep breath. "Lopex, I know you're concerned. Sending us up there was a mistake. But those men are gone. We have to cut our losses and sail now, before those lions of hers get hungry. Or she finds us herself." His words seemed calm, at least for Ury, but his voice held a strange undertone. I risked a peek from behind the head of the ship.

Ury was leaning on his crutch just down the beach from the ship. Lopex was facing him, arms crossed. "You're very quick to abandon the men I entrusted to you, Ury," he was saying softly. "Surely they deserve an attempt to save them. Let's wait and see if any come back." He cocked his head. "Do you hear something?"

Ury glanced around quickly as Lopex continued. "Someone's coming." He turned back toward where I was hiding. "Whoever you are, come out!"

I stepped out from behind the ship as if I had just arrived. Ury's eyebrows shot up. "You!" he snarled, his expression lurching through surprise and rage before settling on something meant to look like relief. "I mean—good, boy—you've escaped!"

Lopex spoke before I could answer. "Perhaps I was too quick to promote you, Ury. I hope this will teach you not to be so eager to abandon your men, even your slaves. Your men are safe, and the sorceress has sworn an oath not to harm us. I have come to fetch the rest of the crew. We will camp on the beach while we refit, and take our meals at her cottage." Just before he turned away, his gaze rested on my face for an instant, and one eyelid twitched. I watched him walk away, but there was no further sign of recognition, and I dismissed it. Surely Lopex hadn't just winked his thanks at me.

As we headed back inland, Ury grabbed me. To anyone watching it would have looked like he was leaning on me, but with each step he squeezed my neck painfully. "That's the second time you've made me look a fool, boy," he muttered, his beard scratching my ear. "I won't forget it. Lopex wants you alive, but you don't need your tongue. I wouldn't go to sleep if I were you, slave."

For the next few days, the thought of a furious Ury with an even worse grudge had me glancing over my shoulder at every noise, but his leg kept him from acting on his threat. Meanwhile, Lopex seemed to be everywhere at once, choosing trees to shape into replacement oars, working with our fat stores-master to replenish our ship's provisions and chivvying the carpenter to complete repairs to the *Pelagios*. On the fifth day after we reached the island I saw Lopex returning to the beach from somewhere. The ship's carpenter, a balding little man with only three fingers on his right hand, was sidling up to him, shaking his head.

"It's not so simple as all that, Lopex," he was saying. "A month'll never do, not with the state she's in." He leaned down to rap at a hull plank near the sand. "D'you hear that? Half these planks, it's just barnacles and shipworm holding them together. And the deep waves, they flex her keel fierce as she crests. It's Poseidon's own miracle that we haven't all fed the eels, sailing her like this. Now, back at Korinthos yard I could refit in a month, but here I'll have to cut and shape every-thing separate." He shook his head, sucking air through his teeth. "You don't want to rush it, Lopex. It's her knees, don't you see, her knees won't take it, they're hanging off their pins—"

Lopex held up a weary hand. "Stop." Caught in mid-flow, the carpenter looked up.

"Just get it done quickly. I'll assign some men to help you," Lopex went on. "As for parts, Circe will provide whatever I want . . ." His voice trailed off as he stared up the hill in the direction of Circe's cottage.

All at once his gaze returned to the carpenter. "You're right, Arturos. This is too important to rush. Take whatever time you need. I will take it upon myself to ensure that the sorceress stays friendly to us." He turned and headed back up the path toward Circe's cottage. Perplexed, the carpenter stared after him, rubbing the back of his neck.

On a cloudy morning over a month later, I was finishing some supper leavings with Zosimea, a sharp-tongued older woman who had been enslaved with me at Troy. From down the beach, I could hear the crack of wood against wood and some half-hearted cursing. At my glance, Zosimea shrugged. "Some idiot Greek thing, boy. Don't get involved." I got up and headed closer to see anyway.

On the far side of the *Pelagios*, two men were practising sparfighting, brandishing wooden poles at one another like swords, surrounded by a dozen watching men. The trainer was a wiry, nut-brown man they called Pakullos, fighting in nothing but a loincloth and sandals. He must have had at least fifteen years on his opponent, but he was leaping about like a monkey, skipping easily out of the way of his opponent's spar while landing blow after blow himself. Thersites, a slope-shouldered Greek soldier with a foul temper, was going to be badly bruised tomorrow. I slipped quietly between a couple of cheering Greeks to watch.

"Hit me, you oaf!" Pakullos was squeaking. "Not like that, are you throwing flower petals? No, never look where you're striking, your eyes give you away. Always look at your opponent's face, you bumbling *sueios ekpneusis*!"

Even after a year with the Greeks, that insult took me a moment. I ducked my head down to hide my smile as I got it, but Thersites, leaning on his spar for a breather, spotted me.

"Think this is funny, slave boy?" he snarled. "Laughing at me, are you?" He threw his spar at me and I caught it automatically. "The slave, he's going to show us how it's done!" he shouted.

I was about to drop the spar and run off when a hand pinned my shoulder. "If you run now, you know, they'll never respect you," Deklah said softly. "Pakullos will give you a few falls. You're small. Just try to be hard to hit." He gave me a shove that sent me staggering into the ring.

Pakullos eyed me dubiously and looked back at the circle of men. "Spar with *that*?" he called, disbelieving. "What's next —a cripple?" Already worked up, the men kept shouting, and Pakullos turned back to me with a grunt. "All right. This won't take long. Let's see your clay, boy." Suddenly I was on the ground, my right shoulder throbbing. What had just happened? I stood up carefully.

"Have to be faster than that, boy." Pakullos was standing a few paces away, waiting. I took a step toward him and suddenly found my face in the sand again, this time the throbbing in my left shoulder.

"Useless. One more fall and you can go." Pakullos sounded bored. Over the noise of the men I could hear Thersites jeering loudly.

Suddenly it was very important not to let Pakullos hit me

again. I had to parry at least one strike. *Be hard to hit.* He was fast, but he wasn't an immortal. I climbed slowly back to my feet but this time, instead of holding my spar at the end like a sword, I gripped it in the middle, my hands a waist-width apart. The Greeks wouldn't do this because it was useless for attack, but I was interested only in defence.

Suddenly Pakullos was darting at me again, his spar swinging toward my neck. I whipped one end of my spar up to block his before it could connect and it whistled past my ear. He was caught off guard but recaptured his balance instantly, stepping back and retaining perfect control. I'd stopped him! I kept my spar crossways in front of me.

Suddenly he was directly before me again, his spar raining blows from all directions at once. I had a quick eye and reflexes—I'd needed them to knock seagulls from the sky, back in Troy—and found myself parrying frantically. With this grip my spar could spin to block almost instantly, and aside from two deflections that glanced off my ear and knuckle, nothing landed.

Pakullos stepped back. He didn't look bored anymore. The catcalls of the Greeks had fallen silent. Suddenly he came at me again, staring fixedly at my shin, his spar lining up for the strike. I spun to parry, but—*never look where you're striking.* At the last instant I raised my spar and parried his actual strike, a wicked slash to the head that could have knocked me out if it had landed. Unprepared, he lost his balance and staggered backward. He was open! I took a step to follow up with a strike against his unprotected side, but stopped, suspicious. Sure enough, the moment I stopped he sprang back into balance. It had been a trap. A murmur ran around the watching soldiers.

I braced myself for another onslaught but he planted his spar unexpectedly in the sand, looking at me thoughtfully. "Not bad, shrimpling. Good clay." As I turned to leave the ring he called after me. "Come by some time, Trojan. We'll try you out on sword and shield."

Later that day Deklah came up to me as I was returning to the camp with firewood. "I think you've earned the right to carry this, Trojan," he said, holding out a knife. It was my sister's, the one he had taken from me among the ship breakers.

We spent another two months on Circe's island until one morning, collecting the breakfast platters to carry out to the Greeks, I saw Circe and Lopex emerge from her cottage. She had a concerned hand on his arm. "Promise me, my sweet?" she was saying. "Especially about the island of Helios? If you don't . . . I wish the entrails were clearer, but . . ."

He nodded gravely. "I give you my word we will do as you have said."

She brightened. "I'll prepare a special farewell banquet for your men tonight. But right now, do you think we have a little time for ourselves?"

That afternoon, Lopex strode onto the beach to announce that the ship's repairs were done at last. "And tonight," he added as the men gathered, "Circe will provide us with a feast to honour our brave companions who were lost at the island of the ship breakers."

The next morning I was set to work loading stores into the hold. It had rained in the night, and the deck and ladder were still slippery. In addition to the standard supplies of millet, olive oil and cured meat, the list of stores included two live sheep, fodder and, strangest of all, a large bundle of tarred greenwood torches. Last night's feast had included several large amphoras of dark Pramnian wine trundled out around the courtyard, and I had a dry mouth and a pounding headache this morning from a long night of wine testing. Or perhaps just drinking, my memory was hazy.

As I yanked another sack of millet from the cart and hoisted it onto my shoulder, I spotted Pen hanging around anxiously by the stern ladder, looking mournful. Well, whatever the problem was, it was his sour water, not mine. As I carried the millet sack over, I could feel his eyes on me with each step. He sighed as I approached.

"Hi, Alexi." His lower lip was split and puffy.

I just waited. He sighed again, louder. "Alexi?" he began. "Aren't you my friend?"

Oh, gods. "Look, Elpenor," I grunted, the millet sack growing heavier by the moment, "I'm supposed to be loading stores. Do you want to get off this island or not?"

He eyed me reproachfully. "I guess you were having too much fun with your new friends last night."

I squinted, trying to draw the evening back through the fog of wine. Someone had asked me to sit at their fire. Deklah, Pharos, Adelphos . . . I vaguely recalled people handing me meat and bronze cups of wine. Lots of laughter, and the drunken insults that the Greeks considered high wit.

"Why didn't you stop them? They would have listened to you." His eyes glistened like a puppy's. "They respect you now."

I stared at him. The barest hint of a memory from last night stirred uneasily in my gut but I pushed it away. "Stop who? What are you talking about?"

He shrugged. "It's okay. Now that you're friends with the soldiers I guess you don't need me around anymore."

Friends? What—"Pen, look, Hades curse it," I burst out, my shoulder aching beneath the heavy sack. "Can't this wait? My arm's about to break off."

Pen's eyes filled with tears. "I'm sorry, Alexi. It's just that . . . you do know that nobody else will talk to me, don't you? I just thought—" his voice broke and he rubbed his eyes with his fists. "I mean, I hoped you were still my friend."

"Boy!" Ury's bellow carried across the camp. "Dump that *nothos* and get back to work!" I spun around to see Ury crutching furiously across the sand. I turned toward the ladder but Pen clutched at my tunic. "Please, Alexi," he said. "Can we talk? Maybe when you're done?"

I sighed. "Fine. As soon as this cart is loaded," I said, watching Ury approach. "But right now, just let go of me, okay?"

Pen dropped his hand and I made for the stern ladder. Lately Ury had taken to balancing on one foot and smashing me in the head with his crutch, but he still couldn't get up the ladder without help.

As I carried the millet sack down into the hold I tried to remember what had happened the previous night. There had been the usual insults, or even more. As I dropped the sack to the floor, a memory surfaced. I'd been carrying platters of pork around to the Greeks, passing Deklah, who didn't eat pork, when something caught in my legs. I tripped, spilling the platter across the sand. Sprawled by the fire, I looked back to see Ury glaring in satisfaction as he pulled his crutch back.

"Club-footed fool," someone hooted. "Are you Trojans all this clumsy?"

A familiar rumble came from the other side of the fire. "More respect for this one, I think, Grathes." It was Pharos. "But for him, you would be now food for the ship breakers."

"This slave?" Grathes eyed me doubtfully.

Pharos nodded. "His warning it was, that alerted us first. And more, his rope and oar pulled you from their grasp."

Grathes stared at him. "*Him*? You pulled us in. I saw you!"

Pharos shrugged, his huge shoulders moving like a landslide. "The strength was mine, but the idea his. Do not discount such a one, even a slave."

Grathes looked at me for a moment. "That was your idea, boy?" I nodded reluctantly, unsure whether to admit it. Since the event with the winds, I'd tried to avoid attention, and this wasn't helping.

"Sure-footed thinking, boy." Taking my arm, he led me

around the fire to a spot on the log beside Pharos. "Sit here. From here on, you eat as one of us."

Back inside the *Pelagios*, I slumped against the stack of millet sacks, overcome by the memory. Had that really happened, or was the wine blurring my memory? And then what was Elpenor so unhappy about? I strained to remember.

Wait. It was coming back. From the far side of the fire, Ury had been glowering like a volcano, shooting fiery glances in my direction, but I'd hardly noticed. Sitting between Grathes and Pharos, sharing the meat and wine and finally joining the conversation, I had felt a warm glow building that had nothing to do with the fire. I'd even told a joke or two that were pretty white-haired in Troy, but new to the Greeks.

Then—that was it. Furious, Ury had grumbled for a while, but then spotted Pen, sitting alone. Yanking him to his feet, Ury had begun cursing at him, forcing him to rinse the spilled pork in the water pail and offer it around. He'd torn off Pen's sandals and thrown them in the fire, making him walk barefoot. Drunk, the other Greeks had watched at first but eventually joined in, jeering and throwing things. First bones, then rocks. Somebody had caught him in the face with a stone, and as he staggered, someone else had tripped him. He had sprawled in the sand nearby.

Pen was right. I could have stopped it. Right then, they would have listened. But what had I done? Nothing. I winced at the memory. Flushed with the pleasure of being accepted for once, I'd looked away, pretending not to notice.

Ignoring Ury's angry shouts, Pen had scrambled up and run off into the darkness, crying. I leaned heavily on the stack of millet sacks, sickened. Since Aeolia, I had known what it was like to be rejected. How could I have done that, and to Pen of all people? I shook my head. From now on I would treat him better, starting by meeting him as I'd promised. And if the Greeks thought less of me for it, so be it.

It didn't work out that way. The cart finally emptied, I was creeping off around the stern to go and find Pen when I came face to face with Ury. "Where are you headed, boy?" he sneered, cuffing me. "Get back to work, you lazy Trojan filth."

I dodged a second blow and went back. It was nearly noon before I found another chance to slip away. Pen wasn't in camp, so I ducked into the woods, searching quietly for a while before spotting a fold of cloth behind a tree.

"Pen?" I called. "Is that you?" There was no sound. "Pen? I wanted to tell you I'm sorry," I added, picking my way through the thicket around the tree. "I've remembered what happened last night." I paused. "You're right, I could have stopped it. I was afraid they'd hate me too. I'm really sorry."

"Pen?" Still no reply. "Please come. I said I was sorry. The ship's nearly ready to sail." I stopped short as I came face to face with him.

He was lying on his side on the ground. For a moment, I thought he was asleep, but his eyes were open. His hand gripped a plant with a strangely shaped purple flower. My grandmother used to keep a pot of them on a ledge outside our door, until my father had noticed them. It was one of the few times I'd seen him angry. I'd been too young to understand, but I recalled him saying something about "deadly poison." And the plant name, *akonitos*, "death without struggle."

I hoped you were still my friend. Pen's words drifted back to me in the still air. How long had he waited here for me, wondering if I was going to show up, before finally giving up? Had he found the poison first and sat here with it, or gone looking for it only when he thought I wasn't coming? Sweet Hera.

Fighting the impulse to curl up into a ball, I picked him up as best I could, easing his body onto my shoulder in a carter's carry and heading back down toward the beach. My path was taking me past the cottage when I heard footsteps tramping through the brush nearby.

"What have you got there, boy?" Ury emerged from the brush with Aegyptos, the solid, one-armed man who had been in charge of the slaves at Troy. Ury peered at Elpenor. "What's his problem? Cry himself to sleep again?"

"Asleep?" I shot back. "He killed himself!"

Ury's eyes grew round. "Trenched himself, did he?" A smile split his face and he elbowed Aegyptos in the side. "Couldn't take the company of men, eh? Or did he just miss his mama too much?"

"No!" I snapped. "I mean, he killed himself . . . by accident." At least I could keep them from dishonouring his memory. "He, uh, fell off the witch's roof. Broke his neck." It wasn't a hero's death, but it was better than suicide.

Ury hooted. "Fell off the roof? Little fool. Useless in battle, useless on an oar. Now he can be useless in Hades. Drop him."

I opened my mouth to argue but stopped, realizing where I was. *Be found never, outside of camp.* Exactly what Pharos had warned me about. Ury's eyes narrowed as he realized the same thing. I thrust Pen's body at him and tried to run but he smashed his crutch against my leg.

"Grab him, Gyp!" he shouted. Aegyptos's big hand seized me hard around the neck. Ury limped up beside me, hand reaching for his knife, when Aegyptos spoke.

"Your father, he was that Trojan healer, right? Him it was, gave me this," he grunted, twitching the stump of his right arm in my face. Beside me, Ury was hissing in excitement as I struggled to get free.

"Stop that, *Trojan*," Aegyptos frowned, giving me an impatient shake. "This, you have to be told. Wouldn't feel right, otherwise. Now listen. It was the second Scamander battle. I'd fallen, pinned by a dead horse. My arm, it was mangled," he said slowly. "Crushed by hooves, torn open by a chariot wheel behind." Ury reached for me but Aegyptos blocked him with his elbow.

"I lay out on the field all night. The Greeks, they didn't find me. Good thing, too—a Greek healer would have nicked and left me dead. Your father it was, he found me, sunup the next morning. By then I was mostly dead anyway."

Aegyptos paused. "I thought I was headed to Hades for sure. Either he'd kill me or my wounds would. But that's not where my road was to go. He gave me some water and tied off my shoulder. Then he took and sawed off my arm. It hurt like four furies. I thought I was dying. It's thanks to him I didn't."

Aegyptos held me at his remaining arm's length and looked me in the eye. "Since that day, I've owed your father a life. Now it's repaid. Get lost." He released me with a shove as Ury spluttered, and I ran for the safety of the camp, leaving Pen's body where it lay.

CHAPTER SIX

The Mouth of Hades

WE PICKED UP THE coastline and followed it westward for nearly a month after leaving Circe's island. For me, it had been a month of painful guilt. I kept picturing Pen's body lying there on the ground where I had left him. Would he be alive if I'd spoken up? Or even listened to him that morning? I didn't know, but the thought gnawed at me constantly.

Two days ago, Lopex had ordered the navigator to the stern and taken over piloting the *Pelagios* himself, gazing fiercely at the land to starboard between glances at a sheepskin chart. Just before noon today he'd shielded his eyes to peer at a misty peak inland and shouted an order. Two men had leapt to furl the sail as Zanthos turned our prow in toward the coast. At the benches, the men extended their oars and began to row for the mouth of a nearby river, spilling from a valley off the starboard bow.

As we entered the valley, the water began to look . . . different. From my usual place on the foredeck, I leaned over the forward rail to watch it slip silently past our keel. If this was water, it was like none I'd ever seen. Black as moonlit blood, it clung to the oars as they pulled free and dripped like slow oil off the blades.

I shivered, watching the bubbles stream past the bow of the *Pelagios*. The pacekeeper's flute piped a slow counterpoint to the regular creak and splash of the oars. My gaze wandered forward and I drew a sharp breath.

A calloused hand clamped over my mouth. "Shut it, boy. The men haven't seen it." Lopex had crossed silently from the far rail and slipped up behind me the instant I'd raised my head. His hand fell away as I nodded and I stared upstream, the black water below us forgotten.

Squatting over the river ahead, a dark, sharp-edged cloud filled the entire valley. I glanced up at Lopex, expecting him to order a halt, but he turned toward the broad backs of the Greeks on the rowing benches behind us and spoke up.

"Men of Ithaca! We will soon be entering a shadowed land, as foretold by the sorceress Circe. With her foreknowledge, I can keep us safe. Nonetheless, if any man here fears the dark, let him show it now by shipping his oar. A slave will take your bench while you rest in the hold." His heavy hand thumped my shoulder. "Otherwise, keep your tongue still and your oar pulling."

I stared at his back. Me, pull one of those huge oars? It took me a moment to realize he was using me yet again. Of course. No soldier would admit being scared now. I looked forward to see the black curtain as it seemed to swoop toward us. I squeezed my eyes tight but a clammy rush told me the moment we entered. My eyes opened again slowly.

The first thing I noticed wasn't the darkness but the colours: there were none. The bright red sash around Pharos's arm had become a dark grey. Near my feet the bow firepot, normally a shiny bronze, was ghostly pale, the fire inside now flickering a cold white.

Behind me, the Greeks muttered at their oars. I braved a glance over the bow rail at the shore. Leafless black trees reached for us from both banks, curls of clammy mist drifting between their trunks like wraiths. Their roots clung to black rock that swirled as though the stone had once flowed like water, while long tendrils of ropy vine hanging from the branches clutched at us as we passed.

Nearby, Lopex was ordering two men up to the bow to hack away the vines that threatened to foul the oars. Glad of the distraction, I watched them leaning out over the rail, cursing as the dark sap oozing from the twitching stumps tarnished their bronze and stung where it touched their skin. Around us, the land was silent, the only noises the slow, thick splash as the oars sliced into the river and the grunts of the men as they slashed at the vines. There were no birds, and it was no wonder. If there were a land less inviting to living things, I doubted mortals had ever seen it. Or come back, if they had.

A few nights earlier, when Deklah had asked where we were headed, Lopex had said only that he had to consult Tiresias, the seer. When I relayed this remark to the other slaves, Kassander had looked surprised. "Tiresias the Theban? I thought he was dead."

Staring around at the brooding, lifeless land around us, I had an uneasy feeling that he was right.

In that twilit place, time was hard to tell, but it might have been late afternoon when the rowers finally pulled us into a tiny lake, scarcely an arrow's flight across, at the head of the river. Its murky surface was half hidden by writhing curls of mist. On three sides, the shoreline was crowded with twisting, dead trees, while on the fourth, a sheer cliff face stretched up from the water to vanish into the gloom above.

Standing in the prow at the very front of the ship, Lopex peered at his sheepskin map. "This is no grove," he muttered. He broke off as he saw me watching. "Find something to do, boy, or by the gods I'll find it for you!"

I dropped down the ladder into the hold to fetch oil for the bow fire pot, although it didn't need it. The olive oil was stored in a clay *pithos* in the bow, and as I reached in with the dipper, Kassander came up behind me. "Alexi, we need to talk."

"Stay away from me, *Greek*," I grunted, putting the lid back on the *pithos* and heading for the ladder. Kassander was a Greek traitor, hiding out from his countrymen as a Trojan slave.

"Alexi, I know you don't trust me," he said quietly, "but the Greeks are going to get home to Ithaca sooner or later. When that happens, we'll both die. Ury will kill you, and the Greeks—" his voice dropped even further, although we were speaking Anatolean, the language of Troy "—they'll figure out who I am. We need a plan."

I stopped halfway up the ladder. "You're a liar. Why should I believe anything you say? Get away from me, *Arkadios*," I added, spitting out his Greek name like a curse.

His eyebrows rose. "Not that name!" he whispered urgently. "You know what they'll do if they hear it!" I shrugged and continued up the ladder as though I didn't care, but it wasn't true. I wanted to believe him, especially what he had told me about my sister Mela, but I didn't dare.

As I emerged on deck, Lopex was ordering the men to circle the lake, his big hands gripping the rail as he peered at the shore. Whatever he was looking for, he couldn't find it, and after a couple of circuits, he had the ship stop in the centre, the bow facing the cliff face. The men leaned on their oars to hold them out of the water, muttering to one another at their benches. I rested against the rail and looked out at the trees. Was it my imagination, or were those dead limbs reaching for us?

There was a sudden draft, and something appeared at the corner of my eye. I turned to look but there was only the cliff face, and I turned back. A moment later it was there again, like a whisper I couldn't quite hear, hovering at the very edge of my vision. I spun to look once more, but again there was only the rock wall.

I glanced toward the Greeks. Had anyone else seen it? They were talking quietly on their rowing benches, facing the other way. Lopex was studying his sheepskin chart, his back to the rail. The navigator and the steersman were having a quiet conversation at the stern. Nobody was looking this way.

There it was a third time, a cold draft on my back. This time I turned slowly, forcing my gaze to fix on the trees to starboard. The draft was now at my side, as though it was coming directly out of the rock face. Struggling not to turn, I studied the rock as well as I could from the corner of my eye.

At the very edge of my vision, something was opening at the base of the cliff wall, like a huge eye—or a mouth. Startled, I turned to look but it was gone, vanished as if it had never been. A shiver ran down my back.

"What are you looking at, boy?" Silent as ever, Lopex had crossed from the port rail and was standing beside me, staring out at the trees. I kept silent.

His fingers grabbed my arm painfully. "If you're hiding something, by Athene I'll make you wish you hadn't. What is it?" he growled. I bit my lip and said nothing.

He dropped my arm, then looked into my face and said carefully, "I should have known. A *nothos* like you has no place among men. Get below with the other slaves."

Stung, I pointed. "I saw something. Over there." *Kopros.* How had he made me do that?

He stared impatiently at the rock face for a moment. "Don't lie to me, boy. There's nothing there."

I glared back. "I'm not lying!" I snapped, tensing automatically to dodge a blow, but he just waited, fists on his hips. I glanced around and pointed to a tree on the shore, half concealed by the drifting mist. "Look there. Don't look at the rock face. Just at the edge of your vision. No, don't turn your head. Watch for something to appear in the cliff."

He might have been proud and bad tempered, but he was quick. After a moment his bushy eyebrows shot up. "By the gods!" His voice sounded awed. "Just where it should be. Big enough to sail into!" His brow furrowed as he turned toward me. "Why shouldn't I look at it?"

I hesitated. "I think it's only visible if nobody's looking."

He turned to face the rock, and blinked as it vanished, then turned back to face the tree again. After a moment, the slight draft resumed. He nodded to himself. "The question is, which is real?"

I hadn't thought of that. He climbed down into the hold and returned with his bow. Stringing it in a single casual motion, he fitted an arrow and let fly. It cracked against the rock face to tumble down into the water. His jaw tightened.

"That's it, then. The cave is the illusion. The rock face is real."

So that's what I was seeing, a cave. I frowned for a moment. What about the draft? And why—"That's not right," I blurted.

"Who would create an illusion we can't even see?"

He squinted at me. "Mind the tongue, boy. And talk sense."

I swallowed. "What I mean is—if the gods wanted to destroy us, wouldn't they make the cave the illusion, and hide the cliff? That way we'd row right into the rock face."

"You saw my arrow, boy. That rock is no illusion."

"But what about the draft?" I licked my dry lips. "The cave and the cliff, I think they're both real. But the cave is only real when nobody's watching."

Lopex looked at me thoughtfully. "You might have something there, boy. Can you prove it?"

I paused. "Line up another arrow for the cave, then close your eyes and shoot. The arrow should go into the cave if you're not looking."

He shook his head. "I have to see it myself." He paused. "I hear you have a good arm, boy. Can you get something into the cave mouth without looking?"

"I think so." My throwing arm had been trained by countless squirrel and seagull hunts back in Troy.

"Stay here." He dropped into the hold and emerged a moment later with a goblet and a rag. I recognized the embossed lion-and-owl insignia on the side. It had been looted from the palace at Troy. Well, King Priam wouldn't be needing it now.

He handed it to me. "Wrap this and light it, then throw it into the cave. I'll look to the side and watch where it goes. Don't light it until I say."

He turned to face the men behind us, still sitting on their

benches, their backs to us. A few had turned and were watching us idly. "Men!" he said loudly. "Look to the shore!" He pointed astern, at the shore on the far side from the rock face. "Over there is the portal we seek. A gold drinking cup to the first man who sees it!"

Their heads whipped around to peer through the mist at the twisting trees on the shoreline, and he turned quickly back to me. "Throw it, boy, before they look back."

I bent to light the bundle in the bow fire pot, then stood up and stared at the tree off to starboard. After a moment, I could make out the black mouth again at the very edge of my vision. Could I do this without looking? Gripping the rail with my left hand, I lined up as best I could, and threw the bundle hard to the side.

At the far corner of my eye, the flaming bundle fluttered toward the cave mouth and vanished into the blackness inside.

CHAPTER SEVEN

Drawing the Shades

THE CAVE WALLS WERE smooth and round, like the lair of some huge earthworm. A pale grey light came from all around, giving the fabric of our tunics a strange glow. We weren't even rowing—as the bow of the *Pelagios* had penetrated the cave, the waters of the lake had begun to draw back into the tunnel, swallowing us with it down a throat barely wide enough for the ship. Our steersman was straining at his steering blade to keep us away from the walls as the oily current drew us further in.

The black water beneath us was as smooth as ever, but the ship was gradually tilting downward, picking up speed until we shot out into what looked like a small underground lake, no more than two arrow flights across. Our momentum carried us past chariot-sized lumps of what looked like half-chewed meat, until we crunched to a halt on the gloomy shore opposite.

Lopex's voice cut through the nervous mutters. "We're here. Ury, we'll need picks, shovels, white barley, a full wineskin . . ." His voice faded as he headed down the ladder and into the hold.

They hadn't been ordered to, but most of the men were buckling on their sword harnesses. Not for the first time, I wished I had one too. Just where had he brought us?

The men had the same question, nervous anger growing in their voices as we assembled on the pebbly shore. At Lopex's command, they had brought out a strange collection, including torches, both fire pots, several tarred faggots of green wood, and strangest of all, the pure white ewe and the black ram that we had loaded at Circe's island.

"Is it not obvious?" Speaking from the bow railing of the *Pelagios*, Lopex overrode their grumbles. "We have descended to where no living man born of woman has ever been: the land of the dead. We are in the underworld realm of Lord Hades himself."

Dismay flickered through the knot of men.

"Hades? You've brought us to *Hades*?"

"Hera's holy halter, what were you thinking?"

"Sweet gods, how will we get out? Great Zeus, please help us!"

I could see why Lopex hadn't said so before. The men would have sliced him up in a heartbeat. Even now, his chances looked poor. Fear turning to anger, the men were reaching for their weapons.

Lopex spoke again. "Heroes of Troy!" His commanding tone quelled them for an instant and his voice thrust into the gap. "You are under a curse!"

He had their attention now. The men stared up at him, wide-eyed.

"It was the sorcerer Circe, by whose art this was revealed to me." A mutter ran through the men. "Yes, a curse. For your part in destroying the city of Troy, you are all fated to die. The gods who could not save Troy are determined to vanquish you, the victors." He paused, permitting the men's frightened clamour to build for a few moments before speaking again.

"But Circe revealed as well how you can avoid your fate. On your behalf I will undertake it. Alone, I must speak to the shade of the seer Tiresias. Only he has the knowledge to stay the curse."

His voice rose over their clamour once more. "I speak the truth. This is the only way home. And the story of this adventure will make your legs welcome under any table, or in any bed, beneath the eye of Helios." He left them no time to think. "Now follow me."

Climbing lightly down the boarding net, he headed up the beach into the dead, colourless land beyond. After a moment of indecision, the men followed in a tight knot. I trailed behind, holding a bronze-bladed shovel before me like a weapon.

Lopex himself was tugging the two sheep along by their halters, the ewe shining eerily white in the strange cave light.

The beach gave way to a sticky moss that smothered the rock beneath, glowing with a pale light that turned black where the men had trodden. In the gloom around me, wispy shapes writhed and twisted at the corner of my vision, retreating when I turned to look. *Hades.* A cold shiver ran down my spine. Those writhing shapes—were any of them people we once knew? The men bunched tighter as we continued inland.

"Halt!" Lopex had stopped, holding a lit torch over his head like a beacon. "This is the place." A wide, black river lay before us, oozing past between steep banks of smooth clay. Lopex scraped two marks a man's height apart in the moss above the bank. "Those of you with shovels, I need a trench between these two points. Do *not* let the river touch your skin."

I shuffled forward reluctantly and began to dig alongside the others, but the clay beneath the moss was too hard for me to penetrate. The other diggers were throwing their clods into the river where they vanished beneath the oily surface without a ripple.

An elbow took me hard in the back and left me scrambling for balance. I lost my footing and slipped over the lip of the bank, my heels gouging ruts in the slick clay slope as I slid toward the water. I turned to grab at the bank but the glowing moss tore out in loose clumps.

A hand reached down and grabbed me under the armpit.

"Fall not, into that river." Pharos's deep voice rumbled near my ear as he lifted me one-handed back onto the turf. He plucked the shovel from my grasp and took over my digging.

I glanced around to spot Ury glowering at me nearby, his black eyes full of hate, and backed away nervously until I bumped into a boulder. That had been no accident. I'd never understood why Ury hated me so much. I had been mouthy with him a few times, but his hatred came from something deeper. Looking at the dark water he had nearly pushed me into, I felt my legs grow weak and sank onto the boulder. Kassander was right about one thing. Someday, Ury was going to kill me.

With Pharos's help, the short trench was complete, and Lopex filled it with wine, then slit the throats of both sheep and drained their blood into it, carefully avoiding the spatter. I glanced over at a shout from one of the soldiers. The dead land around us was suddenly crawling, swarming with . . . a cold sweat broke out on my forehead. *Wraiths.*

Cold candle flames guttering in an unseen breeze, the dead souls of the underworld twisted and drifted over the barren ground. Something was drawing them to us. The Greeks automatically formed a tight circle, their backs to the trench, swords waving anxiously as the wraiths pressed in on them from all sides. Shadowy forms slipped past me on the rock mound, heading for the men around the trench.

Too frightened to move, I huddled where I was, but the wraiths were ignoring me, drifting toward the fresh blood.

Nearby, Lopex stood up with a bundle of freshly-lit pitch torches and caught sight of the swords. "Put those away," he barked. "You think you can cut a wraith? Torches of green, living wood are what they fear. Now keep them from the trench. This offering is for one alone." As he came past he caught sight of me perched on the boulder and stared wordlessly for a moment before handing me a torch. The shades shrank back beyond the circle of light as he handed out the others.

My stomach had knotted itself into a fist. I wanted to get up and join the soldiers but didn't trust my legs. Just beyond the circle of torchlight, thousands of shades flickered and sighed, pressing in wherever the torchlight faltered. If those torches failed . . .

"Tiresias!" Lopex's voice boomed out through the gloom. "Show yourself! Drink your fill at the blood sacrifice we have prepared, for you alone!"

One of the wraiths detached itself from the flickers beyond the firelight and writhed closer. Lopex waved the torches off to let it approach. The men moved aside hastily as it drifted toward them. Above the trench, it stopped, twisting in the rising fumes of hot blood and wine.

I watched, amazed. As the wispy thing basked in the scent above the trench, it began to solidify. One moment I could see the dull glint of Adelphos's sword through it; the next, I could not. I rubbed my eyes. The wraith was gone, and a frail, pale old man with pure white skin, hair, and long cloak was standing knee-deep in the trench where it had been.

"Tiresias of Thebes!" If Lopex was nervous, it didn't show. He strode forward and reached down to take its arm. "I am Odysseus, son of Laertes, destroyer of Troy. I have crossed the seas with one goal: to venture into Hades to seek the advice of the great Theban sage Tiresias, whose fame as a seer is undiminished even by death."

I grunted. Our misfortunes hadn't soured his tongue any. As they walked past my seat on the boulder, I caught a little of their conversation. Tiresias's high-pitched voice crackled as he spoke.

"... yes, yes." I heard his impatient grumble as he shuffled past, Lopex's firm grip on his arm. "And I'll bet you think daisies grow out of my *gloutos* too, don't you, sonny? You young sprouts are all the same, all honey tongue and hurry. Well, make it quick, I'm a busy man. And that wine you used, what was it, vinegar? It makes my skin itch. I knew the man you call your father, I'll be seeing him again soon enough. *He* wouldn't be shoving an old man along like this, I can tell you ..." His crackle faded as they moved off.

I looked up in dismay as the hissing greenwood torch in my hand guttered and went out. The tarred tip had been consumed, the wood too green to burn on its own. Over by the trench, the Greeks had stood aside now that Lopex had accomplished his goal. Wraiths were converging from all directions. I recoiled as one of the drifting wisps paused before me. It seemed to be struggling to hold a shape. The shape of a man. No, a boy. I peered at what might have been a face. From the writhing half-lips came a whisper like wind through bulrushes.

"Alexi, my friend," came a half-imagined sigh. "Is it really you?"

I froze. "Elpenor? Pen?"

Did it nod? The lips parted again, but I couldn't make out the words. The sorrowful almost-face contorted in an intense effort and its voice became clear for an instant. "Bury me. Bury my body."

His wraith whispered something more but the sounds were indistinct, as if the effort had exhausted it. I glanced over at the trench, where hungry ghosts were flowing over and under one another like coiling snakes, basking in the fumes. My gut knotting, I blew on my smouldering torch and coaxed a reluctant flame from it, then slipped off the boulder.

Gesturing for Pen's wraith to follow, I headed for the trench, holding the flickering torch before me like a sword. The wraiths drifted apart, and Elpenor's ghost slipped almost apologetically between them to stop above the trench. As he hovered above it, he seemed to thicken and solidify. One moment I was looking through an insubstantial wisp, and the next at the white form of Elpenor, still clad in the *chiton* he had been wearing when I found his body. He stepped out gingerly, his body and clothing still pale white, somehow untouched by the bloody mixture in the trench.

I opened my mouth, fidgeting for something to say, but he

found his voice first. "Thanks. I could never have gotten there before the blood cooled. Even dead, the strong ones push the rest of us around. Especially the unburied."

A surge of guilt lanced through me. I had abandoned his body, unburied, in the forest. I risked a glance at his face but his expression was innocent.

"It's the life force in the blood," he was saying. "It draws us. Human blood would be best, of course." A white tongue flickered over his lips as I took a step back, almost tripping over a heavy pickaxe that one of the Greeks had dropped. "Sorry," he added. "Do you mind if we talk about something else, Alexi?"

Good idea. "So, Pen, have you—" I floundered for something to say "—met anyone you know?"

He seized on it gratefully. "Oh, yes. There are plenty of Greek soldiers down here. We're drawn to the people we knew in life. There are Trojans too, but they won't talk to me. Well, neither do the Greeks, much."

A chill ran up my spine. Would Sophronios be around somewhere? It had been the Cyclops that had killed him, not me, but I doubted he'd see it that way. I bent to grab the pick I'd tripped over and started along the bank of the black river, heading away from the trench. Pen trotted eagerly along beside me.

I took a deep breath. "Pen? There's something I need to say. I'm really sorry. About the night of the feast. And your . . . death. It's just—"

Pen gave a nimble shrug. "I understand. I know you would have stopped them if you could. You were afraid they'd go for you too."

Gods, was he trying to make me feel worse? I wanted him to shout at me, to show some anger, but he skipped on happily. "It's my own fault, really," he added. "I wasn't supposed to be here. With the war, I mean. A year ago, when my father sent a ship back for the spring recruits, I was only fourteen, but I stowed away on my father's ship, with my brother's armour."

Pen had never said any of this while he was alive. Perhaps he would have, if I'd been listening. As if reading my guilty thoughts, he added, "I don't know why I didn't tell you this before . . ." He shrugged, embarrassed. "Well, you know." He pointed ahead at the round hill I'd seen earlier. "Want to see something? Come on, I'll show you. The view is better from the top." Lopex still seemed occupied with Tiresias, so I followed Pen to the top, breaking a sweat in the humid air.

Looking down the far side I could see a granite boulder, tall as a man and worn perfectly round, halfway down the hill. As I watched, it rocked and shifted slightly. *Uphill.* Pen glanced over shyly as though showing me a secret. "Do you know what that is?"

I watched as the boulder inched its way up toward us. "Uh, Pen, shouldn't we get out of the way? At least I should. I guess you're in no danger—" I broke off as I realized how tactless that sounded, but he didn't notice.

"Don't worry. We're safe here."

The boulder crept its way up the hill toward us, and now I could hear wheezing from behind it. "Someone's pushing it!"

Pen nodded. It was almost at the top now, nearly close enough to reach down and touch. I was getting nervous but Pen seemed unconcerned. A gruff voice was panting, "Nearly there . . . this time . . ."

Suddenly the boulder slipped to the side and began to tumble back down the hill. "Gods curse it!" came a despairing shout. "Not again!" It picked up speed and crashed down the hill to rumble to a stop not far from the bottom.

I glanced at the man who had been behind it. Heavy and bald, with short, powerful arms and bowed legs, he stared up at us. Give him more hair and less paunch and he'd look something like Lopex. "Curse all the gods, I nearly had it that time. Better leverage, that's what I need." He turned and stumped back down the hill.

I looked at Pen, who shrugged. "All I know is, he hasn't stopped since I got here. But he's special, he keeps his life form. There's a few like that. They say his name is Sisyphus."

I glanced back toward the Greeks. Lopex was still deep in conversation with the seer. Down the hill, the stocky man put his shoulder to the rock and began pushing it up the hill again. "Hey!" I called. "Why are you doing that?"

As if on cue, the boulder leapt from his grasp and rolled back down. He glared up at me, panting. "Now look what you've done, curse you!" He gestured down the hill. "I nearly had it!"

He'd been hardly a quarter of the way up, but I wasn't about to argue with someone who could push a boulder uphill. Even if he was dead. "Um, sorry." I walked down the hill after him, Elpenor trailing anxiously behind. "Why are you doing that?"

He reached the boulder and glanced at me. "Something I did," he muttered. "Doesn't matter now. But Zeus hates me for it, may his *kopros*-befouled beard catch fire. Should have known he had no sense of humour. Anyway, this is my punishment." He gave the rock a kick. "Once I get old Berta here to the very top, I can stop."

"So why do you keep letting go?"

"You think I'm doing it on purpose?" he grunted. "You try pushing that gods-cursed thing up a hill, boy. It's enchanted. As soon as I get near the top, it slips to the side and gets away."

Uh huh. "So why don't you try something else?"

He gestured impatiently around us. "Look around, boy. See any carpenter's shops? Nothing to build a ramp out of, scaffolding, winches, not even wood for a rolling channel. And no tools anyway. So I keep trying. Maybe one day Hades will be distracted, curse his flea-ridden armpits, and the enchantment will collapse for just long enough."

You didn't meet many people willing to curse the gods like that, and I found myself liking him. I looked at the boulder for a moment, thinking. "Does the boulder have to be in one piece?"

He squinted at me. "In one piece? What do I look like— Herakles? Just how am I going to break it up, boy, chew it to bits?"

I hesitated for a moment before holding out the pick I'd been carrying. "I was just thinking—maybe you could use this."

He drew a breath to argue, then stopped, frowning. "Bring it up in pieces?" He scratched his chin through his beard. "You know, son, that just might work. Nobody said it had to be intact." He swung the pick experimentally at the boulder and watched a large flake chip off, nodding thoughtfully.

"Listen, son, you've done me a good turn. Let me return the favour. From up here I see everything. You came in through the lake portal." He gestured at me with the pickaxe. "I tell you this: getting in is hard, but getting out is worse. Hades, curse his filthy feet, lets nothing escape. In my time I've seen every exit this place ever had. As he finds them, he seals them. If you're thinking you can just row back out, think again."

I nodded. We'd shot down that channel like an oat down a throat. I couldn't see us getting out that way again.

"Just remember, boy. You're in Hades now. Hades the god, Hades the domain. He won't let you go." He caught my puzzled expression and bent down to look me in the eye. "He has to want you out. Irritate him, boy. That's your escape."

Hefting the pick, he added, "Now stand back; I've got some gravel to make."

As we returned to my boulder near the Greeks, I glanced over at Elpenor. To my dismay, he didn't look solid anymore, his sharp edges fading. "Pen? What's happening?"

He held up his arms and I realized with a shock I could see

through them. "It's the blood meal. It doesn't last. I should have sat still." Why hadn't he said something? He was reverting to a shapeless wisp before my eyes. A formless hand reached for my shoulder but passed through it like a cold shiver. What remained of his face contorted as he struggled to speak. "Remember, Alexi." His voice was a fading whisper. "Bury my body. Please. And watch for the dead ... the dead you knew ..."

His voice faded into a reedy whisper, and the wisp that had been Elpenor drifted away on an unfelt breeze.

I stared after him, willing him to come back, but he was gone. I turned slowly and made my way down the hill to the Greeks and perched on my boulder again. Lopex was talking to a group of shades in armour.

What had Pen meant: watch for the dead I knew? Sophronios, of course. I shuddered. Stupid to have given away that pick. If that creature got his hands on me now, he'd kill me and spend eternity tormenting me. Somehow I was sure he would have been one of the first at the blood trough.

There was movement out of the corner of my eye. A shade had left the few still sipping the last cooling fumes at the trench, slipping toward me across the rocky ground. I sprang to my feet, but as the grey form came closer, I spotted a pale arrow sticking awkwardly out of its chest. That was strange. Sophro had been killed by the Cyclops, his head smashed against a wall.

The figure loomed out of the gloom. It was a man, slimmer

than Sophro, wearing a simple *chiton*, no armour.

I knew him. Gods, I knew him. I swallowed, fighting sudden tears.

"Father?"

The shade slipped up to me and stopped. "Alexi? *Son*?"

CHAPTER EIGHT

Fleeing the Dead Lands

MY MOUTH OPEN, I couldn't make a sound. Suddenly I had my arms around him, a strange, cold sensation, but I didn't care. It was my father. His voice murmured in my ear. "Lex, Lex. I'm so sorry. You know I would have given anything to stay with you." A cold afterlife of the arrow that had killed him was rubbing awkwardly against my neck, but I didn't care.

He steered me back to the boulder and we sat down side by side. "We don't have much time, son. The spirit meal will give me substance only for a little while. So tell me, what are you doing here?"

My father! As if a floodgate had opened, I began to talk, holding nothing back. The three years after his death on the battlefield outside Troy, three years in which Melantha and I had bartered everything we owned for food. Being thrown out of our house to become street orphans. The fall of Troy, after the Greeks somehow got inside the city walls.

He shook his head. "Past the walls? That can't be right. Nothing got through those walls, not in seven years of siege."

I grunted. "Look, I didn't say I knew how. But I was there. You were—" I broke off.

He nodded heavily. "I'm sorry, son. I wish ... well, you know what I wish. I'm glad you've survived, at least."

Melantha—he didn't know. I moved on quickly. "They used some sort of trick to get in. I don't know what. We thought we'd won! The day after they left, the whole city held a party in the streets. We were wrong, though. The Greeks had all sailed away, but that was a trick too. The whole fleet came back that night, when everyone was drunk or asleep."

My father had glanced over at Lopex at the mention of a trick. I nodded. "He had something to do with it. Or so he said. He was the one who took me as a slave. I suppose I should be glad. Ury was about to kill me."

My father rubbed his mouth thoughtfully. "So you're a slave now?" I nodded. "At least you're alive. If you want to survive, make yourself as useful as you can, perhaps as a healer's boy. And for Athene's sake, Alexi, *try* not to talk back."

"If you hadn't gotten yourself killed, you could have trained me," I snapped. The words were barely out before I wanted them back. "Father, I—"

"Alexi, you don't know—" he said at the same time.

I found my voice again first. "I'm sorry, father," I said. "It wasn't your fault."

He sighed. "No, you're right. If I hadn't been out on that battlefield, perhaps I'd still be alive."

"I guess." That reminded me. "Do you remember a Greek soldier, a big man, bald, bulging lower lip, named Aegyptos? He said you took his arm off on the battlefield."

My father thought for a moment. "I didn't know his name, but yes, that sounds familiar." He nodded. "I remember now. It was during the second battle of the Scamander plain. His arm was mangled, half ripped off. The wound filled with mud from the plain. Likely it saved him from bleeding to death, though. I never heard if he'd survived. Why?"

"Did you know you saved my life that day?"

My father looked at me, puzzled, and I described how Aegyptos had saved me from Ury to repay the debt. My father's eyes were glistening as I finished. "Well." His hands brushed his ghostly *chiton*. "Well," he repeated. "Son, I'm so glad. You don't know how I've felt, leaving you. I'm glad you told me."

Suddenly he frowned, tilting his head.

"Father?" I asked. "What—"

He put up a hand. "Listen."

Around me, the background whisper of the milling shades was swelling, becoming shrill and anxious. No longer drifting aimlessly, they had begun to flitter and dart about in agitation.

My father had his head tilted up, listening. "The shades are disturbed. I can feel it too. It's something . . ." his eyes focused and he gripped my arm. "Alexi, you'd better leave. Right away."

"What is it?" I began, but broke off. From the distance came an eerie howl that could have escaped no mortal throat. The back of my neck prickled.

"It's *him*." My father's tone was urgent. He gave my forehead a quick, cold kiss as he hauled me to my feet, then shoved me after the Greeks, already edging nervously toward their ship. I turned back to say goodbye, but he shook his head. "Just run. Don't look back." As I started after the departing Greeks, he called out. "May the gods be with you, son. I know you'll make me proud."

There was a sound like the crack of a monstrous whip, and another unearthly howl ripped the air apart behind me. Ahead, the Greeks broke into a run, leaving dark footprints in the glowing moss. I put on a burst of speed, darting through a curtain of frantic shades to reach the beach just as the ship pushed into the water. As Lopex went over the bow rail, he turned back to frown at me for a moment before reaching down to haul me up and drop me sprawling on the deck. "Phidios!" he called to the rowing master as he turned away. "Take us across! Find the entrance!"

As the men bent their backs to pull us across the dark lake, I looked back. Coming around the hill I had climbed earlier was something huge. A monstrous, malformed dog-shape, wrinkled and hairless as a newborn rat, as big as the *Pelagios* herself. Its pale skin was crisscrossed with slashes and half-healed scars. As the creature emerged from behind the hill on its stubby legs, the welts oozed a deep, glowing red, shocking to the eye in this land of grey.

It reached the top of the hill, squatted and raised its snout to unleash a deafening howl, shot through with rage and pain. Another howl joined the first, and I peered through the gloom before spotting the source: hanging like a tumour off the creature's bloated belly was a second head. As it turned its lacerated snout to bay in our direction, I caught sight of a third head, hairless and long-nosed, snapping rat's teeth at us from deep inside the creature's mouth.

Facing backward to row, the men had a clear view of the creature and were pulling hard enough to bend their oars. Ahead, the portal we had come down was coming into view through the gloom. But dry! The water that had swallowed us down had drained away, and the channel sloped upward.

The bald man with the boulder had been right. There was no escaping this way. Wait—what had he said? *Irritate him. You have to make him want you out.* But how did you irritate a god? I was pretty sure shouting insults wouldn't work.

A whip cracked behind us and there came another howl, this one tinged with agony. I turned to see a huge, man-shaped figure towering over the monstrous rat-hound, a whip in his hand. His skin, hair and tunic were utterly, completely black. Not just dark-skinned, as I'd seen on some of the fierce Ethiopian fighters who had been our wartime allies, but an absolute black that soaked up any light falling on it like a sponge. Only his eyes had colour, burning the deep red of live coals in their sockets. A chill ran through me. *Lord Hades.*

The whip cracked again, burning another glowing weal across the dog-creature's hairless flank. It howled its pain and anger once more and began to shuffle down the beach toward us, its belly nearly dragging on the ground.

Make him want you out. My father used to mix salt and mustard to persuade sick stomachs to release their contents. A pity we couldn't force Hades to swallow a dose. He'd spit us out for sure. Or could we? I looked at the rounded walls of the cavern and back at the rocky throat we had come down, thinking—and suddenly I had an idea of what Sisyphus might have meant. Hades the god, Hades the domain. The way he'd said it made it sound like there was no difference.

I leapt down into the bow hold, jarring my shins. There. An urn full of salt. The Greeks used it to preserve their meat for travelling. Snatching up a jute millet sack nearby, I tore it open with my sister's knife and emptied it onto the floor.

Kassander, hidden in the hold, emerged from between two bales of sailcloth. "What is it?"

There was no time. "Hold this." I handed him the sack and tipped the urn into it, then took it from him to lug it back up the ladder to the deck.

Behind us, the creature had nearly dragged itself to the beach. Lopex had stationed archers at the stern, but to that thing, arrows would be no more than flea bites. Phidios had halted us at the upward-sloping entrance to the tunnel, and the rowers muttered apprehensively as the creature approached the water.

I poured the heavy sack over the bow rail into the black water below and watched. Nothing. My heart sank. Looking around at the stomach-like cave, I had been sure this was what Sisyphus had meant. I had already turned away in disappointment when a sudden hiss like a pot reaching a boil drew me back to the rail.

The water off the bow was beginning to bubble and spit. A round, frothing crater was somehow growing in the water next to us. A man's height across one moment, wide enough to hold the ship a moment later. The *Pelagios* lurched sideways as we were pulled over the lip. Still expanding, the crater became a wave, flowing out in all directions from us, growing and frothing. It struck the beach behind us and rebounded, swelling into a churning mass higher than our prow.

At the stern, Lopex could see it coming. "Rowers! Ship oars! Ship oars!" he shouted. "And as you fear the gods, *hang on!*" I dropped to the deck and wound my arms tightly through the bow rail struts. Gods, what had I done? I could hear the wave growing louder as it roared toward us. For a moment it towered over the stern before lifting us like a leaf and thrusting us back up the throat of Hades.

The ship smashed against the tunnel walls as the water threw us back up, snapping off oars and carrying away entire hull planks and railings. Behind us, the roaring black wave filled the entire cave, threatening to engulf us at any moment. My arms were being pulled off my shoulders as I clung desperately to the struts, praying to the gods to hold the ship together. I couldn't even see the last few feet of the stern, swallowed by the rushing black wave. Was it already gone? The Greeks were moaning in terror, and I clamped my mouth hard to keep from doing the same.

Suddenly it was brighter. A moment later we shot out of the tunnel like a cork squeezed from a goatskin, twisting in mid-air to smash down on the water, heeled halfway over in the middle of the grey lake. For a moment I thought the impact had ripped my arms off. The ship bobbed unsteadily, then slowly righted. If we had rolled over and sunk right then, no one could have raised a finger to stop it. As I lay panting, looking back at the solid rock wall I knew we had just been vomited from, my mind returned to something I had glimpsed just before the wave carried us into the tunnel: the huge Lord Hades, bent over the hill and retching, as though he had swallowed something he couldn't digest.

"Why, Lopex!" Circe chirped as he splashed onto the beach from the shallows, her bird's-nest hair bound with a kerchief that matched her robin's-egg blue robe. "What a nice surprise! You couldn't keep away from me after all!" She reached out playfully to take his arm but he yanked it away.

"Not by my choice, witch!" he growled. "No sooner had we departed the river of Hades than a sea current snatched up our ship, a current that we could neither row nor sail against until it beached us here. Do you stand there and tell me it was none of your doing?"

She pouted at him. "Oh, don't be that way." She reached out to brush his hair from his forehead but he frowned and pushed her hand away.

"Please, don't be angry with me." Her face brightened. "And look at your ship, my wolf, you really must stay and repair it. What *have* you been doing to the poor thing? It looks like owls have been nesting in it. Tonight I'll prepare a banquet for you and your men, and read the auguries again to see what else might be in your future." She stood on tiptoe to whisper something in his ear, her hands on his chest. This time he didn't push her away.

That evening, as I approached the soldiers' campfire, I heard Deklah, speaking with his mouth full of bread. "It's true, she didn't even chew her own food. Had a slave do it for her." At someone's question, he added, "No, it wasn't a poison taster. She actually had a food chewer. Spooned it right out of her mouth into the queen's."

The mention of poison reminded me of Pen's death. Pen! I stiffened, remembering my promise. A glance at Ury told me he was too drunk to be a danger to anyone but himself. Even so, I was careful to slip away without being obvious. Grabbing a bolt of sailcloth from the hold as a shroud, I headed for where I had left Pen's body.

The moon, a few days off full, was the kind we called a

trencherman's moon, back in Troy. It was high overhead by the time I found Elpenor's body, lying under a bush. Whether by some magic or the dry island air, it was barely decomposed, and the lions hadn't found it. Wrapping him in the sailcloth, I wrestled him over my shoulder and staggered off in search of a burial site.

I knew it as soon as I spotted it, a moonlit cove a short walk north of the *Pelagios*. A few night gulls wheeled above the moonlit water. An unthreatening scene, the kind Pen would have liked. Buried properly here, perhaps he would have the respect in Hades that he had never had in life. And perhaps the guilt that had eaten at me since his death would finally be appeased.

I laid him in a depression in the hard soil and began to hunt for rocks to build a cairn over him when I realized I wasn't alone. I leapt to my feet, afraid that Ury had followed me after all, but I was wrong. It was Lopex.

I grunted, annoyed. If he didn't like what I was doing, he could do it himself. To my surprise, he said nothing, watching in silence as I covered Pen's body with stones to keep out the animals. As I completed the cairn, Lopex stepped up beside me with a broken oar from the scrap pile. He wedged it, paddle upward, in the stones as a grave marker. We stood side by side for a little while, looking at the grave in silence. "You've done right by him, boy," Lopex said at last. "None of my own men thought to." Confused, I said nothing. He turned and left.

I stood for a little while longer, looking at Pen's grave in the cool night air, but my calm had been broken. Why did he keep doing that? Ever since Aeolia, I had hated him. He had given me away to Ury. He had used me, when we first landed on Circe's island, to make the men eat. He wouldn't let me speak to him, and when he spoke to me it was only to give orders. And I couldn't forget that he was one of the Greek commanders who had destroyed Troy. He made it easy to hate him. So why did I find it so hard?

We spent another month on Circe's island, refitting the damage done during our escape from Hades, but Lopex didn't speak to me again. For this refitting, although it looked bad, the damage was almost all minor, mostly railings, oars, and a few stove-in hull planks. I had no carpentry skills, something that became clear when Arturos pressed me into service turning new oars. After examining the misshapen result, he'd looked at me sourly and told me he didn't need me any longer.

Following breakfast one day, I crept off to hide in the shade of the *Pelagios*. The Greeks had propped her up on the beach with two rows of ashwood stay poles, forming a kind of triangular tunnel against each side of the hull. The side away from camp was almost out of sight, so I was a bit surprised, as I settled into place with my back against the hull, to look up and see Thersites standing there.

"You're the son of that healer, right?" he began. I nodded.

"I don't much have dealings with healers, you understand," he went on awkwardly. "Not slaves, neither. But Pharos, he says you're okay. And they say you saved some men at the ship break island. Is that the way of it?"

I nodded again, wondering where this was going.

He glanced over his shoulder before squatting in front of me. "See, it's like this," he began, his voice low. "I've gone and got myself a rash."

"A rash?" I repeated, surprised.

He turned his back to me and flipped his tunic up. His buttocks and the backs of his thighs were speckled bright red. He let his tunic drop and turned back. "Thing is," he added, "I'd just as soon you didn't let on to the others, see? Only they'd pin my ears pretty fierce for falling asleep in a patch of foolsnare like that." He stood up again.

"Word is, you've got a healer's box. If it's got something to keep the itch down, well, I'd count it as a good turn." He grimaced and whipped a hand around to scratch urgently at his buttock. "Only hurry," he hissed. "This itch, it's growing to eat me whole."

The healer's box! Binding wounds and splinting bones didn't need a healer's elixirs, and I'd long since forgotten the box I had last seen on the island of the Cyclops. It took a while to find it, buried in the hold where some soldier had heaved it.

A wave of nostalgia wafted over me as I threw open the lid. The neat rows of stoppered clay vials, the mortar, pestle and other tools in the bottom, and above all the scent of herbs, liniments and tinctures rising from the box carried me back to the days when I used to help my father in the *xenion* where he treated his patients.

The vials were marked with neatly scratched labels, but I'd never learned to read, so I started opening them at random. Some contained oil with chopped leaves in them, others powder or balms. One had a piercing smell that darted up my nostrils like a wasp. I put the stopper back hastily.

Finally I found a vial full of a thick oil with a flowery scent that I half-recalled my father smearing on someone's burnt arm. Could it help? Did ointments go bad, like food? I didn't know. I poured some into a smaller vial and brought it out to Thersites. "Spread this on twice a day. It may help, if it hasn't stopped working."

I didn't hear back from Thersites, but a day later another Greek soldier came to me, a younger man named Prylis. "Listen," he began. "I hear you've got something for an itch." He held up his forearms, which were red with signs of vigorous scratching. "Can you give me a little? I can't even sleep these last two nights."

Word must have gotten around, because after that, the men began coming to me with a stream of burns and minor injuries, giving me an opportunity to experiment with the other salves and tinctures in the healer's box. Through trial and error, I began to identify what some of the ointments and powders were good for. By the time we set sail from Circe's island again after a month, I understood what at least a third of the vials in the healer's chest were for. From the men's grudging comments, that made me at least as good as the Greek healer I had replaced, the late and unlamented Kallikrates.

CHAPTER NINE

Peril on the Water

PROCOROS HAD A CONFUSED frown. "*Toward* it? Don't you mean *around* it?"

Standing beside him at the bow rail, Lopex was studying his sheepskin chart. He glanced up at the late morning sun, now emerging from behind a scrap of cloud. "Hold this course," he repeated. "The island will come into view within two hands. Bring the ship close by, keeping the island two oar-lengths to starboard. Under *no* circumstances are you to land us."

The navigator muttered into his beard. At the water halt a little while later, Lopex ordered me to hand out a thumb-sized piece of beeswax to every man on board. I'd wondered

about it the day before when I saw it in the hold as we prepared to leave Circe's island. Whatever we were about to meet,
Lopex already knew about it.

He hadn't mentioned the slaves, but I dropped a lump
down the forward ladder into the hold anyway. Zosimea, I
had learned after we sailed, had been left with Circe as a gift.
The half-dozen other slaves we had set out with had been re-
assigned to other ships after the Cyclops island and lost at the
ship breakers, leaving only me and Kassander aboard the
Pelagios. As I worked my way down the benches, handing out
lumps of wax to the rowers, Lopex spoke up from the stern.

"Men of Ithaca!" he called, holding up a lump of beeswax.
"You are being given a piece of wax. Roll it in your hands to
soften it and fashion yourself two plugs, like this." He dem-
onstrated. "On my command, push them into your ears. As
you value your lives, make sure they are tight, and do not re-
move them until Phidios gestures to you. Ury, bring up the
mast from below. Leave off the sail and spars."

Unimaginative as always, Ury stepped up from the forward
rowing bench where Lopex had relocated him after Circe's
island, and gruffly ordered four men to the task. They wrestled the mast from the hold and struggled with its stay ropes
to mount it through a collar hole in the bench. I finished
distributing the wax and reached the stern deck just as Lopex
was telling Phidios to tie him up.

I blinked. Had I heard that wrong? From the look on his
face, Phidios was wondering the same thing, but Lopex was

thrusting a coil of ox-hide rope at him. Phidios uncoiled the rope gingerly and reached for Lopex's arms.

"Not here, idiot. To the mast!" At least that explained why he had asked Ury to raise it. The men watched with interest as Lopex was bound to the mast, facing to starboard, his feet on the reinforced bench that housed the mast hole. He raised his voice. "Fellow Achaeans, I charge you all: no matter what you see or hear, and in particular no matter what I say, do not untie me until we are safely past the island." He turned to Phidios. "Tighter! There must be no chance for me to escape."

I thought about this as the men began rowing again. What sort of danger was best met tied up? And why weren't the rest of us being bound too? I shrugged and hopped across the benches to my standard spot in the bow. Lopex ignored me as I passed.

A shout came from Procoros. "There it is! Steersman, alter your course to my mark!" He pointed a steady arm toward a spot on the horizon as the ship gradually swung around.

I watched from the bow rail as the island crept closer. Could I hear something? I strained to catch the sound, a low, sweet throbbing. Lopex's voice boomed out again. "Plugs! Now!" I stuffed the wax plugs into my ears and the world became nearly silent, the creaking of the ship and the waves against the hull muffled.

The men resumed rowing at an arms-out gesture from Phidios. As we drew nearer to the island, I began to make out details. Thrust jaggedly up from the waves, it was more of an outcropping than a real island. Sharp-edged rocks lined the base of the sheer cliffs that protected it on all sides, and scattered among notches in the cliffs were some half-dozen . . . creatures.

Now I could make them out. Women! Beautiful women with long, dark green hair that shone like seaweed draped over their shoulders to run like rivers down smooth, silvery skin. Their mouths were open as though they were calling. No, singing. With my ears plugged I couldn't hear their voices, but their open-armed, graceful gestures were clear.

"Come! Visit with us!" Facing backward, the rowers couldn't see them yet, but our course would take us directly past them, a stone's throw to starboard. I glanced back at the men, wondering how they would react, and was transfixed as I caught sight of Lopex.

His head was turned toward the island, and his face bore an intense expression that might have been rapture or agony. His lips were moving as he muttered something, his face working, sweat beginning on his forehead. His mouth opened and I realized that the voices must be growing louder. I crept down the benches until I could make out his words through the earplugs.

". . . music . . . wrong . . . let me go . . . voices of gods . . ."

Suddenly his eye fell upon me and his voice raised to a shout. "You! Come here! Yes, you!"

I hesitated and his shout came again. "Boy! Now, may the gods damn you!"

I bench-hopped over uncertainly as Lopex continued to curse.

"Untie me, slave. Now!"

I stared at him in amazement. "But you ordered us not to!"

Lopex glared at me, panting, sweat running freely off his face. "I said untie me!"

I looked at him innocently. "I'd love to, but you're not my master anymore. Remember?"

His face twitched as he fought to control himself. Suddenly his expression changed, a cunning look stealing over his writhing brow. "Oh, yes. Ury." He was struggling not to shout. "Not much of a . . . master, is he? Tell you what, Alexi. Let me go and I'll make him give you back to me. How'd you like that?"

The singing must have grown louder, for I could suddenly hear it too, a faint humming. Even through the wax, it was beautiful. What would he do if I released him? A brief spasm crossed his face.

"What do you say, Alexi? Ury reports to me. I can order him to. The gods know there's . . . precedent."

I glanced anxiously toward the island, now directly to starboard as we rowed past. This close, I could see broken shapes among the sharp-toothed rocks at the base of the cliff. A momentary breeze blew a carrion smell past my nostrils, and I knew what those shapes had to be.

Lopex was speaking again. "Better still—" a conspiratorial look crossed his face as he leaned toward me, straining against the ropes, "I'll make him set you free! Think of that. Free again!" The crumpled shapes were men, the broken bodies of sailors who had been driven to scale those impossible cliffs by these creatures' music. Now I knew what he would do if I let him go.

Lopex's voice rose as the last of his self-control vanished. "Do it now, boy!" he shouted, straining at the cords, his eyes bulging. "Or I'll make your final days short and full of pain!" His face contorted further as I fidgeted. "You stinking Trojan scum! Do it! Now! I should have let Ury cut out your heart back in Troy, you little filth!"

So that was how he really felt. Could anyone blame me now if I cut him loose? My hand was reaching on its own for Melantha's knife. Lopex watched me hungrily. "That's right, boy. Do it. Do it now," he said, his voice cracking.

I shielded my eyes against the sun as I looked for the main rope strand to cut that would free him. Wait—the sun? It shouldn't be in my eyes. I glanced toward the bow. We were turning directly into the island! I spun and looked backward, ignoring Lopex's angry cry. Zanthos, the steersman, was pulling the starboard steering oar hard in toward the island, a manic smile on his face. Phidios, keeping the rower's pace on his pipes, hadn't noticed yet.

I dashed over the benches toward the stern, kicking the oars to foul them as I passed, but the sailors cursed and recovered their stroke. At the stern deck I leapt to grab Zanthos's arm, but his wiry body was stronger than it looked. As I wrestled with him I spotted the problem: a wax plug had fallen from his ear! I gulped—there was only one solution. I pulled a wax plug from my ear and reached up to thrust it into his.

An immediate change came over his face. He looked up as though waking from a dream, shook his head and hurriedly twisted his steering oar for a sharp turn to port. Nearby, Phidios had dropped his flute and was frantically signalling for the men to reverse direction, but I didn't notice.

I could hear the music now.

Powerful and pure, it flooded through me like sweet wine, setting my entire body thrumming like a lyre string. I had to get closer. I had no more choice than a raindrop has to fall. I was already halfway over the railing when an arm caught me. A voice spoke in my ear. "Easy, boy. They're not worth dying for."

Some part of me recognized the speaker as Zanthos, but I didn't care. If I had been capable of forming any sort of thought I could easily have stabbed him just to get him out of my way, but at that moment my mind could hold no intent but the driving need to reach the source of that sweet sound filling my head.

As I flailed to get free, a lucky scratch caught him below the eye and he cursed, letting go of me to clap a hand to his face. I scrambled back over the rail and was about to jump when his arm caught me again. "Determined little thing, aren't you?" came his voice. "Well, I can't say that I blame you, having heard it myself. But it's no use struggling. I'm not letting you go, no, not till we're well past those creatures."

I continued fighting, but the earlier throbbing desperation was ebbing, flowing back out like a receding wave. The music was fading, the insistent song growing quieter behind us as we pulled away from the island.

I looked down to find myself kneeling on the rail. What was I doing up here? Behind me, Zanthos was holding the steering oar with one hand, his other wrapped tightly around me. Blood trickled down his cheek from a deep scratch.

"Zanthos?" I began uncertainly, memory coming back.

He shook his head, taking his earplugs out at a signal from Phidios. "Don't worry about it, boy," he said. "If you hadn't given me your wax we'd all be feeding the eels now."

I glanced toward the stern. The island was still visible, but the music was almost inaudible, now nothing more than a pleasant hum, an echo of the bliss that had filled me. I shook my head, trying to clear the sweet longing from it, when I realized where I had felt this once before. It was as we left the island of the lotos-eaters, watching it recede behind us, that I had felt the same desperate sense of loss, knowing that a part of me would forever long to return.

That evening we pulled up onto a pebbled black beach, a round-shouldered mountain just visible inland in the dusk. I sat alone for supper that night, hoping to avoid Lopex, but he found me anyway, sitting in a dry creek bed up the beach and gnawing on a slice of dried pork.

"Boy."

I twisted around to see him standing behind me at the edge of the wash, hands on his hips. "Yes, sir?"

"I gave you an order today. You didn't obey."

"Well, no, I—"

"Do you know what would have happened if you had?"

I nodded. "I heard the music too."

His eyebrows raised for an instant and I added, "Zanthos— he stopped me."

"Ury would have become the new commander." Lopex's voice was dry.

Gods! I hadn't thought of that. Ury in command? I wouldn't have lasted a day. Or worse, he might have kept me alive. I stared at Lopex, speechless.

Lopex looked me directly in the eye. "It's a good thing for us both that you disobeyed, then."

CHAPTER TEN

Between Monster and Maelstrom

SOMETHING WAS WORRYING LOPEX. He had been pacing back and forth on the foredeck near me all morning, pausing occasionally to peer at the horizon, hardly visible under a grey sky. A cold wind was whipping spray over the bow from the tops of the waves, leaving the foredeck slick and our clothes damp. Twice Lopex turned as if to address the men as they rowed, but each time he stopped. It was during a water break that he finally spoke.

"Men! Soldiers of Achaea!" he called out as the men lounged on their benches. From where I squatted against the bow rail it looked like he was avoiding their eyes.

He paused. "This has been a long voyage. We have had more misfortune than anyone should have to bear." One of his big hands was twisting an edge of his tunic. He frowned at it for a moment before going on.

"Misfortune," he repeated, staring at his hand. "I wish I could say that it was over, that our misfortune was done. And with the help of Pallas Athene, we may be near the end. The end," he repeated. Gods, he was almost rambling. He noticed the men's odd looks and seemed to collect himself.

"I want you all to know that, whatever happens . . . I have been proud to command you. Whatever dangers we may find, you will face them with courage and fortitude. I will expect nothing less." As he turned away, he added, in a low tone that only I heard, "Athene protect us." His face was as grey as the sky.

He stood at the bow the rest of the morning, gazing at the sea ahead. Behind him the men muttered as they rowed. The sun was hidden, but it must have been around noon when I saw him stiffen. Peeking out between the bow rails, I saw what seemed to be a solid line of cliffs on the horizon. "Set course for that gap," he called to Procoros. "No, there. To port, between those cliffs. There should be a passage there."

As the rowers drew us nearer I began to hear a noise, a powerful gurgling, like water draining through a monstrous sluice-gate. Dead ahead of us, a gap in the cliffs hinted at a way through. I couldn't be sure, because a thick, sea-born mist filled it from one side to the other. Lopex grabbed Procoros by the shoulder.

"As the gods are your guides, keep our course to port, along the eastern cliff. We'll be safe there. Safer." He glanced up at the cliffs to port and turned around to face the rowing benches. "Men of Achaea! No matter what happens, no matter what you see, *do not abandon your oars*. It is imperative that we keep our speed up through the passage. Above all, do not let your oars foul or we will lose headway. Phidios, set the pace to double time." He lowered his voice again and bent his head to speak quietly to the navigator. "Procoros, arm yourself and take up station at the stern."

Watching him, I felt the hair prickling on my arms. Not once, facing the Cyclops, the ship breakers or even Hades himself, had Lopex ever looked uncertain. But now, as I watched him climb out of the forward hold carrying his bow, two spears and his helmet, his expression was uneasy, even anxious. He stalked past me at the bow rail and continued up to the prow to peer forward.

As we sliced into the fog, the sound of the rushing water beneath our keel ceased as though a bronze door had closed. Even the oar splashes were muffled, sucked away into the swirling mist that I watched grow thicker until I could barely see past my outstretched hand. Ury and a silent man named Demetrios were just shapes on the forward rowing bench, their backs toward me, the rest of the ship invisible in the fog. By the bow, I could just make out Lopex's broad shoulders and the crossed-axe emblem on his helmet as he peered out at the sea ahead.

At our doubled rowing pace, the ship was lunging forward at every sweep of the oars, and I clung to the forward rail for balance. Racing through the fog at this shipwreck speed, a cliff lurking unseen somewhere off to port, seemed like six kinds of madness, and I wondered again what could be so dangerous that this was the safer choice.

"Look there! Who saw that?" A shout made me turn. Through the fog I could just make out a figure on the forward rowing bench. It was Ury, his finger stabbing at the fog to port.

"Out there!" he was shouting angrily. "Curse the gods, it's out there!" Peering into the fog, I expected to catch sight of the cliff, but could see only mist. As I stared, there was a sudden sharp crack of wood on wood and a curse from the rowing bench just beyond Ury's. At this high speed the oarsmen needed perfect timing, and two of their oars must have fouled. An extended wooden clatter and a series of oaths ripped from the fog as the remaining port-side oars, their rhythm interrupted, crashed into one another in a wave. The ship's headway slowed immediately and it slewed sharply to the left.

"All rowers! Break stroke!" Lopex shouted. The starboard rowers halted and the *Pelagios* drifted to a standstill in the mist. Striding down the benches toward the stern, Lopex shouted again. "Phidios! Restart us *now*!"

Ury was peering suspiciously out to sea as Phidios shouted from the rear deck to turn the ship and restart the rowing sequence, Lopex relaying his commands forward from the centre bench. The ship slowly began to move again, and Lopex came past me and disappeared into the grey haze as he returned to the bow, spears in hand.

There was no warning. Directly above Demetrios, a huge, green-scaled head lunged down out of the mist, its jaws gaping to engulf his head and shoulders before snatching him up into the air. Demetrios disappeared upward into the fog, legs still kicking. The most terrifying thing about it had been the complete silence—he hadn't had time to utter a sound.

I leapt to pull his oar out of the way, opening my mouth to shout a warning, but caught myself. If the rowers were distracted, the oars would foul again, and it was suddenly clear what Lopex meant—we had to escape this channel as quickly as possible. I unlaced the oar quickly and heaved it up onto the foredeck, hoping the worst was over.

It wasn't. As I leapt back onto the foredeck there was another commotion amidships and a muffled shriek, instantly cut off. Then another, further back, and still another. "Keep rowing! Get those oars clear!" Lopex had returned from the forward rail and his bark cut through the fog like an axe. Already rowing their utmost, the men found new strength in their terror. There was a crack from the fog as an oar snapped under the strain. "Ship the stub!" shouted Lopex. "Maintain your stroke! Pull! Pull!" Backing away in terror, I felt a cold sensation and turned forward.

Nearly beside me on the foredeck, another huge head had appeared silently out of the mist over the starboard bow rail directly between Lopex and me. Hanging above the deck, it slipped past me, turning from side to side, its mouth gaping open, its narrow tongue flickering as it tasted the mist. Lopex, his back to the bow as he pointed his spear into the fog over the rowers, hadn't spotted it.

I opened my mouth to shout a warning but terror had gripped my throat and all that came out was a strangled croak. The head whipped around at the sound and came at me, jaws horribly wide, huge fangs above and below curved inward to pierce and hold. I scrambled backward across the deck and found myself holding the oar before me like a spar. Without thinking, I swung one end around to smash the side of the creature's head. It snapped at it reflexively but released it as it tasted the wood and turned back toward me.

Backing up, I was stopped by the port bow rail as that huge mouth continued to approach. Deep in the thing's oily red maw, ropy muscles lining the throat stretched and rippled, preparing to swallow. Impelled by terror, I levelled the oar at the creature like a spear and thrust the blade of the oar between the fangs and as far down its throat as I could.

The creature stopped its advance instantly, shaking its head to dislodge the oar but it was caught fast, powerful contractions already drawing the oar deeper into its throat. The gods had never designed it to deal with unwanted food leaping into its mouth. Twitching spastically, the head withdrew into the fog and vanished.

There was a sudden gust of wind, and the fog cleared for a moment. We were less than two oar-lengths from a sheer cliff that came down to the water's edge. I scrambled to my feet and looked up to see six snake-like heads dangling down the cliff on impossibly long necks, now withdrawing into a cave high above the port side. Five of them held men, wriggling like fish impaled on hooks. With the mist gone, their muffled screams assaulted our ears.

"Lopex! Sweet gods, please save us! Gods, please!" The sixth head whipped frantically back and forth as it tried to shake loose the oar already drawn halfway down its throat.

The men in the boat stared up in horror. "Sweet Athene, look!" someone shouted. "Lopex! Do something! Name of the gods, save them!"

Lopex dropped his spears and in a single continuous motion plucked his bow from his shoulder and sent five arrows flying upwards. They sank deep into the chests of the five men, who stopped wriggling instantly. The heads retreated into the cave.

He turned back to the men. "I told you to row, gods curse you! That was just a snack. She'll be back soon. Put your backs into it!" Terrified, the men unfouled their oars and began to pull, peering anxiously upward as we passed below the cave, but the creature's heads stayed hidden inside.

There was a roaring from the sea off to starboard, a noise that had been muffled by the mist. I turned to look over the opposite rail and realized why Lopex had taken our course so close to cliffs. On our other side, the ship was sliding past the rim of a monstrous whirlpool. Even as I watched, a broken oar whipped around it to vanish into its dark eye, swirling and sucking only a stone's throw to starboard. Its outer lip was lapping at our hull, while its far edge was up hard against another cliff only a bowshot away. A thick mist streamed from it like breath, spreading across the water to hide it again as I watched.

No wonder Lopex had kept us to this side. Any farther from the cliffs and we would have been drawn into that whirlpool, losing the ship and everyone on board. At least this way we had lost only a few men. Circe must have warned him.

Lopex was fingering a spear as he peered up at the portside cliff, the creature's cave slipping into the mist behind us. I frowned. Circe had warned him? I gasped as I realized what that meant. That was why he had been anxious—he had known that we would lose those men. Even before we set sail, *Lopex had known.*

CHAPTER ELEVEN

Island of the Sun God

"ABSOLUTELY NOT. Under no circumstances will we land here." Lopex was staring down Procoros the navigator, who was glaring back at him, brandishing his sheepskin map. I had poked my head out of the forward hold to watch. Slipping past us to port was a green, lush island. I'd been on board long enough now to know what to look for, and even from here I could see a stream running down into a sheltered beach. With evening coming on, it would make a good drawing-up point for the night.

Ury stood up, letting go of his oar, which began trailing in the water. As it fouled the others, the *Pelagios* lost headway and began to drift. I ducked back into the hold to avoid a kick in the head as he stepped past me onto the bow deck.

"Why aren't we stopping?" he asked Procoros, gesturing angrily to port. "There's a watered beach right there!"

The navigator turned to him. "Lopex won't let us."

Lopex spoke up. "I have good reasons. Believe me, we will be safer."

Ury stared back at him. "Safer? Like we were with that sea monster? Who told you this, anyway?"

Lopex looked impatient. "You know the answer as well as I. It was Circe, the sorceress. All that she has predicted has come true. And she warned me that great harm would befall us if we land on that island."

At the mention of Circe, Ury's voice took on a tremor. "That witch? You trust her? She turned your men into pigs!"

The navigator spoke up. "Lopex, my charts don't show this island, but they don't show any others on this course for a day's sailing either." He sniffed. "The breeze is rising and smells of rain. We need to beach."

Lopex drummed his fingers impatiently on the rail for a moment, then turned toward the rowing benches. "Men!" he said loudly. "We will stop here for the night on one condition. Each of you must swear an oath to me, by the six children of Cronos, that you will do no harm to the cattle that live here."

The men stared back. A nervous laugh came from somewhere. "Cattle? You mean cows? Rrrr-rrrr cows?" someone said, making the odd sound that Greeks thought cows made.

Lopex looked at him seriously. "Yes, Thersites, cows. We

will land only if you swear not to harm any cattle you find here." The men clearly didn't find it that serious, but they swore willingly enough and took up their oars again.

As we rowed in, I was struck by something: the entire island was covered in gently rolling hills, not a rock or gully to be seen amid the blanket of dark green grass. Behind me, one of the rowers had noticed the same thing. "Look at all that grass. You'd think it was pastureland for the gods."

That evening I was sitting on a log by the soldiers' fire between Pharos and a sharp-faced man named Leonidas, one of the men who had come on board after the disaster with the ship breakers. Part way around the fire, Ury had been drinking heavily from a looted gold *rhyton* of wine, muttering and shooting angry glances at me. Draining it in a final swallow, he dropped it and lurched to his feet. As he passed he launched a vicious kick that was probably aimed at my head, but caught the edge of my shoulder.

Pharos frowned. "Harm not our healer, cousin. He may heal you someday, perhaps." Ury blinked at him and staggered off.

Leonidas turned to look at me, shaking his head. "Just can't stand the sight of you, can he?" he asked. "So what did you do, boy?"

I shrugged. "Not much. I told him he stank. Back in Troy."

Leonidas looked quizzically at me. "That's *it*? I thought you'd tarred his beard at least." Hot tar and wine in a drunkard's beard was a Greek favourite. It took days to comb out, and meanwhile the scent drew flies.

Beside me, Pharos let out a long, smoked-fish belch. "More, I think. Our healer lives, where young brother of Ury died. Now Ury seeks Trojan blood for his brother's."

I kept my mouth shut with an effort. It wasn't my fault—the Greeks had invaded us! I hadn't killed his stupid brother, but I'd been just behind him on the steps when my sister had, stabbing him as he hauled her out. In the darkness, the Greeks had thought the person on the steps had done it. Thank the gods they didn't know it was me.

I shook my head. "Pharos?" I blurted, anxious to change the topic. "How did the Greeks get into Troy, that night?" I half hoped he wouldn't answer, but he turned a slow eye toward me, the dying firelight making his face ruddy. "The giant horse. The horse of Troy." His face clouded. "An unholy ruse. Mocking the gods."

Sitting cross-legged on a square of sailcloth nearby, Deklah was drinking wine from a double-handled bowl. He put it down unsteadily, splashing a red stain across the cloth. "Maybe," he grunted, his accent strong tonight. "I'm not proud of it. But if we hadn't, it might have been your bones outside Troy now, Pharos. Have you forgotten we were starving?"

We hadn't exactly been eating turtle eggs and sweet pork inside the walls either. My mouth twisted at the memory of stringy, half-burnt seagull.

Pharos had grunted something and Deklah was glaring back at him. "You know nothing, Pharos!" he snarled. "You think we volunteered? I never wanted anything to do with it! May the name curse that horse!"

The soldier beside Pharos had caught Deklah's last few words. "The horse! Tell us about the horse!" he roared, his face red with wine. Others around the fire picked it up and began chanting, beating time on their knees. "Heroes of the horse! Heroes of the horse!"

Deklah looked at them. "Heroes? You think we were *heroes*? It was nothing like that." He spat. "*Nothing.*" He glared around the circle of firelight but the chanting just got louder. Eventually he held up his hands. "Enough! I'll tell you. But I promise, you won't like it."

He picked up his wine to walk over to a tangle of driftwood stacked near the fire, and stared into his drinking bowl for a long moment. The men hushed one another as he looked up. "First of all, whatever you've heard, we weren't volunteers. We were tricked.

"You remember when King Agamemnon announced that there was no shame being defeated by gods, so after ten years it was time to go home? He was a liar. It was part of a plan that he and Lopex thought up. Why we believed him, I don't know. But we couldn't load our boats and sail for home fast enough. Remember how we even burnt out our camp? We were fools."

He shook his head. "Think about it. When we left Troy that day, why did we set sail so late in the afternoon? I'll tell you. To make sure we'd stop at Tenedos for the night. Nice and close," he added bitterly. "King Ag, Lopex, the other local commanders—they knew we were going back.

"Look around. Do you see Lopex here?" Deklah gestured

around the camp. "Even now, he's too proud to eat with us. So that night on Tenedos when he offered a few of us some wine that he'd hidden away, I thought he was trying to say sorry. For keeping us from home for ten years. For losing the war."

He grimaced and drained his wine bowl. "I don't know what he put in that wine but I woke up in the early morning with eleven other men and a howling headache." There was a stir around the campfire. Deklah had been wrong. If there was one story the Greeks liked better than heroism, it was betrayal. Skewers of dried fish sat in the men's hands or lay forgotten on the sand.

A guffaw came from the darkness just beyond the firelight. "Couldn't hold your grapes, heretic?" Ury staggered into the light, a wineskin perched on his shoulder, the bunghole beside his mouth. "Try praying to that *name* of yours, see if that helps."

He lurched to a stop in front of Deklah. "Heretic!" he slurred, nearly toppling backward into the fire. "Did you hear me? I said, pray—"

Pharos came up quickly behind Ury and dragged him firmly away by the shoulder. "Silence, cousin. Not to look foolish."

Deklah sighed. "So there I am. Around me the other men are just waking up," he went on. "I figure out I'm straddling some kind of long beam, men on it just ahead and behind me. It sounds like we're packed into a small wooden room, perhaps ten or twelve of us.

"Then I hear Lopex behind me. 'Agamemnon's carpenters spent six months building this, out on the island of Tenedos where the Trojans wouldn't see,' he says. 'It's a wooden statue. A horse. When the Trojans spot it at dawn, they'll bring it inside the walls. Tomorrow night, the fleet will return. We will climb out and open the gates of Troy to them.'"

My head jerked up. Gods, please let Deklah be lying. Troy was never taken by something this obvious. King Priam was a little past it, but a giant statue should have made a five-year-old suspicious.

"For a moment I didn't understand," Deklah continued. "Climb out? Then I realized what he meant: *that's* what we were in: a wooden statue! 'It will be light soon,' Lopex said, 'and the Trojans will send scouts. If they hear us inside, they'll burn us alive. One more thing: the hatch is nailed shut from the outside. The only way out now is to get into Troy, where my spy will open it.'"

If I'd still had any hope that Deklah was making this up, it vanished at that moment. Sealing everyone inside with him—so that his plan was their only hope of survival—was the sort of brilliant, dangerous strategy that only Lopex could come up with.

"I could not believe what I was hearing," Deklah was saying. "I tried to turn around, but with the bracebeams left and right it was too cramped. Right behind me, Askrion starts shouting. 'What in *kopros* kind of honourless plan is that? Do you think the Trojans are stupid? What if the fleet doesn't come, or someone farts and the Trojans hear us? That's not a plan; it's suicide!'

"Just behind him, Lopex's voice goes all cold. 'It's like this,' he says. 'If we fail today, we die. The entire Greek fleet can't save us if the Trojans find us.' Then he adds, so soft I can hardly hear him, 'The gods have forced this war upon me. We will win it or die. But challenge me again and you'll never know.'

"Askrion was from Pylos or he would have known better. He shouted something and went to turn around. I heard a knife. Something hot splashed my shoulders, and that bubbling sound, you know, sucking through a slashed throat, and I could smell blood.

"'If we win, nobody will care how we got in.' Right behind me, Askrion is jerking and clutching at me as he slides down. I try to turn and hold him up, but Lopex just keeps talking. 'If we lose, nobody will remember.' Askrion slips out of my grip and slides off the beam behind me. 'The Trojans will come for us soon. From this point on, I will kill the man who speaks without permission.'

"I bit my tongue so hard it bled. We didn't ask for this. I couldn't think of anything except killing Lopex. Even so, at some point I must have drifted off.

"What woke me was a thump. It must have been morning because there was sunlight getting in the cracks. And there were voices outside. Not Greek. The Trojans had found us.

"Lopex hadn't bothered to bring anyone who spoke their

language, but we knew what they were arguing about. Meanwhile it's getting hotter and hotter, sitting in there on the beach as the sun rises. By this time it's gone mid-morning but the sweat-stink is already so bad I can hardly breathe. Nobody bothered building in a place to take a leak, either, so Lopex won't let us drink, only small sips.

"Outside, I can hear a crowd gathering. There's a thump, then some more. They're throwing rocks at us. It's like being chained up inside a drum! Some of the men ahead are moaning in fear. Of course the Trojans aren't going to bring us in. They're going to burn us alive. They're not fools. Then the thumps stop. At first we're relieved. Suddenly there's this huge lurch that throws us against the side—they're trying to knock us over! We brace ourselves as each sway takes us farther. Someone ahead of me throws up, and the smell nearly covers up the sweat and blood.

"Then we hear another voice outside. Greek! The rocking stops. Someone with a Trojan accent starts asking questions. I recognize the Greek voice, it's that little weasel, Sinon. Remember him? The one who was always around when someone's gambling dice or knife disappeared? I guess he stayed behind when we sailed. I can't believe what he's telling them out there. He's saying that Agamemnon tried to sacrifice him for a good sailing wind, but he got away." Deklah sniffed.

"Filthy little liar. That nasty nose-voice of his always made me sick. Next he says that an oracle told the Greeks to build this statue as penance for attacking Troy. The gods would let them sail home if they made it big enough. From the sound of the crowd, they're believing him.

"Finally he says it will protect their city for a thousand years, if they bring it inside." Deklah paused as an owl hooted somewhere inland.

"Pharos, you were right. This was not the warrior's way. Creeping and lying our way in? I wanted to warn them myself. Sinon could never have invented lies like this. It had to be Lopex," Deklah added.

Lopex again. My stomach curled around itself once more.

"Maybe a hand later there's a set of jerks as though we're being levered onto a cart. They turn us around and start pulling us up the hill toward the city gates. The craftsmen who built that thing didn't design it to last, it was just a thin shell. The whole torso is flexing like a child's bow; the stress is pulling it apart. All around me I can hear joints creaking, dowels working loose. I don't even know if it will last long enough to reach the gates. Finally we stop. We must be at the city wall now because I can hear a crowd coming out.

"Suddenly there's a new voice, furious, getting the crowd worked up. Then there's a crunch. Something has smashed into the side. Right in front of me, Stephanos groans and starts to slump down on the beam. A spear has come right through the planking and taken him between the ribs!"

A murmur went through the Greeks but Deklah went on.

"He throws his head back to scream. I reach around and clamp my hand over his mouth, hissing at him to be quiet, but he starts screaming into my palm, jerking and twitching around on the spear.

"Then I realize the whole spear shaft is shaking as he moves. With the other end outside, it's like waving a sheet out a window! I try to hold him still but he's got the pain strength now. Suddenly Lopex is right there behind me. 'Kill him!' he hisses. 'Before he gives us away!' He reaches around and hands me his knife."

Deklah shook his head and looked up at us listening around the campfire, his eyes pleading. "We were about to be discovered. Stephanos would have died anyway, don't you see? Not even our Trojan healer could have saved him. So I took Lopex's knife and . . . pushed it into his ear, where it wouldn't bleed." A murmur went around the fire.

"Stephanos went limp immediately. If I'd let him fall the spear shaft would have moved, so I sat the rest of the day clutching a corpse to my chest.

"Then I hear shouts from outside. Panic. Suddenly there's a scream. Deep, a man in agony. It goes on and on, like it's being squeezed out of him, then a popping noise as if something is being crushed, and the scream drops off.

"There's total silence outside for a while, then I hear that snakeskin voice of Sinon again. 'You see, brave Trojans, how I tell the truth? That is what the gods do to those who defile their gifts.'

"I never found out what happened out there, but after Sinon says this, they can't haul us inside fast enough. It scrapes horribly but they get us in the gates. We can hear the whole city celebrating around us, all day and into the evening. The smells of food and wine just outside are driving us insane. Of course, we've got no food with us, only a little dried fish. The water's long gone.

"It's deep night before it goes quiet. Stephanos is as cold as a dewstone in my arms, and I've been sitting cramped so long I can't even feel my feet. And we're totally blind. Nobody thought to build in spy holes, of course. There could be a whole squadron waiting out there.

"Finally we hear a soft thud below us and that little weasel, Sinon. 'And have the mighty heroes arrived, then?' Lopex just grunts at him to open up. When the hatch behind Lopex finally opens, the fresh air is like the breath of a goddess. I let poor Stephanos go at last and climb out. There's a rope ladder hidden inside a thick fall of horsehair like a giant tail. At the bottom I get my first sight of it, standing on two flatbed carts lashed together, just inside the city gates." Deklah lifted his bowl for a drink, frowning when he found it empty.

"It's a giant horse, just like Lopex said," he continued, dropping the bowl. "The name alone knows what it must have cost. The whole body is polished black maple. The head is so perfect I swear it's looking at me. Eyes of polished marble. Teeth and hooves of beaten gold. You know, the whole Greek army could have eaten for months on what it must have taken to build. Even the tail is real spun horsehair. The thing is glowing like a god in the moonlight. Now I knew why it was so flimsy inside. All the skill must have gone into its appearance. I could almost see why the Trojans were fooled." Deklah's tone was hushed. There wasn't a sound from the men around the fire now.

Deklah frowned. "That's when I noticed where the hatch was. It was right at the end. We had come out through that thing's *gloutos*! Lopex comes around the far side. 'The hatch is there because the tail hides the rope ladder,' he says. He doesn't even sound embarrassed. Right then, we all realize the same thing—Lopex is standing right there, unprotected. We start toward him, but he just looks at us.

"'I wouldn't,' he says, really calm. You'd think he was talking about the weather. 'There's only one way out,' he goes on, 'and that's through those gates.'

"Just then I'm thinking there's another way out, and it's a lot easier. But Lopex continues. 'Right now you're thinking of killing me and running. Just remember, I've got the only weapon,' he says. He pulls out a long knife, very casual. 'A noisy fight will draw every Trojan within five hundred paces,' he says. 'And I promise you, it will be noisy.' He looks around at us. 'Who's first? Neoptolemos? Your father would be ashamed. Deklah? Where's that famous loyalty? Lykos?'

"He licks his lips and his expression changes. 'Believe me when I say I dislike this as much as you do. If I'd asked for volunteers, I would have gotten fireheads and glory-eaters. Men who would betray the mission for their own gain. I chose the twelve of you because you were the best. The smartest.

The most adaptable. Men who would do whatever the mission needed.' He looks right at me. 'You're here because *you're the ones who could pull it off*.'

"He looks around at us. 'We're inside now, and the Trojans don't know it. Beyond those walls, the combined armies have returned to the beach. All we need now is to open those gates and let them in. Go ahead and kill me now. You'll be dead in moments, forgotten by morning. Stand with me, and the story of the horse of Troy will echo for ten thousand years.'"

Deklah shook his head. "If you'd asked me even a hand earlier, I would have sworn we would kill him. But somehow he talked us around. I was there and I still don't know how he did it.

"Under the statue there's a single Trojan guard, dead, a knife in his back with a dozen stab wounds. Sinon has come over, he's hopping from foot to foot, bragging that he brought wine for the guard but stabbed him when he turned his back. Lopex ignores him and starts up the ladder to the watchtower beside the gate. A little while later he's back, splashed with blood and holding a torch. There hasn't been a whisper.

"With the tower unmanned, we set about opening the gates. There are three bronze gate-bolts, each as thick as a man's waist, threaded into giant sockets on the opposite door. We climb up to the catwalks along the back and pull each one out. Thank the name that the Trojans kept them well greased. Even so, it took all of us to shift the bolts. Finally, we heave the doors open. Lopex stands in the opening and waves a torch up and down three times. A little while later we hear the tramp of feet as the army marches up from the beach."

Deklah shook his head in disgust. "This was not how it was supposed to be. We were to take Troy with strength and honour, not by creeping and lying. We were tricked into helping him, and the Trojans into their own defeat. We took Troy, but a thousand years will never wash away the dishonour of how we did it."

So now I knew. Ever since Troy had fallen, I'd wondered. It took me a long time to get to sleep that night.

CHAPTER TWELVE

The Grip of Hunger

AFTER FILLING THE WATER cisterns the next morning, I crept out of camp. Ury had left early with a hunting party, and with them away I wouldn't be missed. The stream I had drawn water from earlier crossed the beach a short walk south of the ship, and I set off for its source, a water skin on my shoulder in case I was seen leaving.

The stream wound across a broad field. After walking for nearly a hand, I entered the narrow mouth of a small valley between two steep, grassy hills that curved like lips around a long, narrow pool. A waterfall perhaps twice my height splashed into it over a narrow cliff at the far end, surrounded by a thicket of dwarf laurel bushes.

The grass was still slippery with morning dew, and as I made my way around the steep-sided valley, I lost my footing and slipped into the water. Once I got used to the feeling of water up to my neck, it was refreshing, and I spent a little while thrashing around, trying to swim.

There was a noise from the bushes behind me.

"Who's there?" I called, turning. When there was no answer, I scrambled out onto the steep bank. Something was moving in the laurel bushes, so I plunged in only to spot someone darting away. I emerged beside the waterfall only an instant later, but whoever it had been had gotten away.

From my quick glimpse, it had looked like someone about my height. One of the Greeks, obviously, but the only Greek close to my height, now that Pen was gone, was Nikias, and he was much heavier. And then there was that noise. Thinking back, it had sounded like something I hadn't heard in a long time—a giggle.

By the time I got back to camp, a wind had come up, a constant breeze blowing off the sea. The hunting party returned late in the afternoon, and I caught their angry tone. "Not a goat or a pig to be found, not even a coney or a curse-eating bird, for Hera's sake," someone muttered, kicking at a driftwood log. A cloud of black and white bees buzzed out but he ignored them. "Nothing but *kopros*-eating cattle. Thank the gods there'll be fish."

But the men sent out with the net in the ship's *skaphis*, the two-man oared boat that the Greeks stored just beneath the stern deck, came back empty-handed too. That night we ate dried fish and millet from storage again, and the men's grumbles took on an anxious tone. "What sort of cursed island is this? Nothing but cattle and grass. The sooner we're shot of this place, the better."

Overnight, the breeze freshened into a stiff wind blowing directly off the water, but soon after sunrise Lopex had us push the ship into the shallows anyway. As the men began to pull their oars, the wind picked up until it was whipping spray off the waves, even in the bay. At full row, the ship was making no headway. "Navigator! Change course!" shouted Lopex. "Angle us away from the wind!"

At the navigator's shout Zanthos obediently turned the ship. The wind pennant at the stern fluttered around as we changed course, but as we stared, it twisted slowly back until it was blowing dead astern again. The wind had shifted to counter us.

"Navigator! Other way!" shouted Lopex. We turned again. This time the change was even swifter, the wind whipping around almost immediately to push us hard back toward the beach. He tried several times, rowing with one bank of oars only, rowing us backwards, even trying to pole us into open water. Nothing worked. It was as if something was trying to keep us there. At last Lopex sighed. "Okay, men. Take us in. We'll stay here for the night and try again when the wind drops."

There was only one problem with Lopex's plan: from that moment on, the wind never dropped. It remained a weak, constant breeze, even at night. The moment we tried to row out, it picked up, twisting to blow us back to the beach. Something was trapping us here, and when the men weren't gambling or squabbling, they began offering libations in the hope of appeasing whichever god might be causing it. Proper meat sacrifices would have been better, but the only meat on this island was out of bounds.

Without fresh provisions from the land, we were rapidly going through our ship's stores. True to their oath, the men hadn't touched the herds of cattle that roamed inland, but they stared at them more hungrily each day. Even with our rations cut to one meal a day, we had long since run out of dried fish and dates, and the remaining two olive oil *pithoi* in the hold had been drained to supplement the men's meals. After about a month, I found myself upending our last sack of musty millet into the cooking pot for the men's breakfast. It was the next morning, with the pinch of real hunger in everyone's bellies now, that things came to a boil.

"Now what?" demanded Ury, hands on his hips, bearded jaw thrust out at Lopex's face. "What's the plan now? Well? Should we go out and eat grass like those cattle you won't let us touch?"

Lopex was unmoved. "It was you who wanted to land here, Ury. I was against it. But now that we have, our lives depend on leaving those cattle alone. We will escape this island only if you do as I say and obey your oath."

"Do as you say?" Ury growled. "That's all we've done. And

look at us! After everything else, now we're starving on an island full of fat cattle! Where's the danger in filling our bellies?"

Heads nearby were turning to listen. Lopex raised his voice. "Men of Ithaca! Ury has asked what harm there is in eating the cattle here. Would you so easily scorn the gods by breaking your oath? The sorceress Circe has warned me that these beasts are protected. If we leave them alone, we will return home safely. Slaughter even one and we will die. This is the fate the gods are preparing for us, the destroyers of Troy, if we fail to respect their wishes now."

"That witch?" Ury sputtered. "How can you believe her? After she turned your men into pigs!" He sounded as if he was about to burst a vein. "Elpenor died there, and you still trust her? Everything that's happened since we sailed has been your fault, Lopex! You're the one who's cursed!"

Lopex, source of the curse? I didn't put much stock in anything Ury said, but that had a rare ring of truth. Regardless, Lopex refused to be drawn. "The curse I spoke of in Hades is real. All that you have seen is proof of that. As for Circe, she revealed many things, and they have all proven true." He raised his voice again. "I will search the island alone and find a way for us to escape. Do as I say and we will all leave safely. On Athene's sacred shield, I give you my word." He went to his tent to collect his spear, then strode off into the hills behind the beach.

That night he was still gone, and the one after that. By the third morning the men were closer to open revolt than I'd ever seen. Among Ury's group, every third word was angry, and only lack of strength kept their arguments from turning deadly. Even Deklah seemed to be trying to pick a fight with Pharos that afternoon.

"*Again?*" I heard Deklah say as I was on my way across the beach, hoping to lick a little oil from the ship's empty fire pots. He was squatting beside Pharos, who was carefully blowing life into a small fire in his pebble-lined offering pit. "Where I come from we stopped worshipping gods like that a thousand years ago."

Pharos's eyebrows went up but he refused to be angered. "Not worshipping the gods?" he replied. "The twelve immortals? Zeus the almighty, Hera his wife. Brothers had he Poseidon earth-shaker and Hades the brooding one. Music from—"

"Names. Names to frighten children," Deklah sniffed. "I've heard you recite that old chant a hundred times, Pharos. The one true god needs no name."

Pharos stared at him. "One god? One god only?" He frowned, thinking. "How to explain the healing and the dying? The rains and the drought, good fortune and bad?" He shook his head. "No, Deklah. There must be many gods, fighting always, bringing us their gifts and curses. This you know."

Deklah scowled. "The one god knows everything. It's not up to us to understand his purpose."

Pharos shook his head again. "Changing his mind always, your god must be, to daily bring such different fortunes."

I couldn't help a smile as I climbed the stern ladder, wondering how I could ever have thought Pharos was simple.

True to his pattern, Kassander had kept out of sight of the Greeks since we'd landed, keeping his head down when he came out for food to avoid being spotted as the man they'd known as Arkadios. As for me, three years as an orphan in Troy had accustomed me to short rations, but after three days with no food at all, the constant ache of hunger was about to claw its way right out of my stomach into the open air. One or two of Ury's angry bunch took to staring at me with the same lean look they used on the herds of glossy white cattle. Like Kassander, I began staying away as much as I could.

Early in the morning of the fourth day after Lopex had gone, I took a walk around the outside of the camp, trying to forget my gnawing hunger. Near the south end of the encampment, one of the island's cattle was standing on a hillside, watching me. Up close it looked rounded and fat, its skin a milky white that contrasted with its coal-black horns. I looked again, surprised. Hanging from one horn was a red bunch of grapes.

I glanced around. Was this some sort of trick? But there were no Greeks nearby, and this wasn't Ury's style anyway. Besides, I was too hungry to care. I reached for the grapes as I came up, but the cow tossed its head and ambled off down the far side of the hill. I glanced around once more and set off after it.

I didn't have the energy to run, but whenever I tried to catch up, the cow broke into a playful trot. Frustrated, I straggled after it. Surely the grapes would drop soon. My eyes on them,

I didn't notice how far we'd come until I looked up and realized we were back in the small valley I'd visited a month ago. We were moving up one side of the valley beside the long pool, nearing the waterfall at the far end.

The cow turned back to look at me, but as I approached, it gave a playful toss of its head, slinging the grapes into the pool. "Hey!" I shouted, leaping into the neck-deep water to snatch them up. At last! As the first sweet grape burst on my tongue, I lost control completely and stuffed them all into my mouth, barely chewing. After four days without food, the relief was so great that my knees buckled, momentarily dunking me. Once I was standing again, I heard a sound from the shore. I splashed in the water for a moment, scanning the stand of dwarf laurels near the water.

There. Someone was peeking out from behind one of the bushes. I could just see part of a face behind a branch. I thought for a moment. The Greeks wouldn't be hiding. Whoever this was, they weren't from the *Pelagios*. And behind that thought came another: if they lived here, they would have food.

The last time I'd been here, I'd tried chasing after them. It hadn't worked. Perhaps this time I could get them to come to me. I climbed out, feeling clammy in my wet tunic, and sat down at the water's edge, facing the pool.

A rustle came from the bushes behind me. I cleared my throat. "Hello? Whoever you are, I just want to talk!"

There was a sound of someone scrambling away through the laurels. *Kopros.* I waited until the noise stopped, then tried again, keeping my tone gentle. "I won't hurt you. I promise."

There was a long pause. I'd nearly given up when a quiet voice came from the bushes nearby. "You won't hurt? Promise?"

"I promise. See, I'm sitting down."

There was a movement in the bushes off to my left. I turned slowly. It was a girl! She was about my age, peering at me out of the bushes, with wide, brown eyes beneath a tight bun of fawn-brown hair. She looked ready to spring back into the bushes at a single wrong word.

"Hello," I said, trying to look harmless. She watched me from under dark eyebrows as if dealing with an exotic monster.

"You're . . . a *boy*, aren't you?" she said at last, pronouncing the Greek word carefully.

I felt my eyebrows shoot up. "Um—yes."

She paused, continuing to watch me. "I'm sorry," she added. "It's just—I've never met a boy before."

I nodded as though I heard this every day. "My name is Alexi."

She looked anxious for a moment, as though this was more than she wanted to know, but then seemed to reconsider. "Mine is Phaith. Short for Phaethusia." There was another silence. My stomach growled, and she tensed again.

"Sorry," I said awkwardly.

"That's okay. I guess you're hungry." She smiled shyly. "Did you like the grapes I sent?"

"You sent them?"

"Gala can be naughty. I'm sorry she threw them in the pond." She took a step out of the bushes and squatted on the ground nearby, staying out of arm's reach. Her tunic came down to her knees, exposing long, coltish legs.

I nodded. "It's okay. I got them. Thanks." Trying to sound casual, I added, "Do you have any more?"

She stiffened. "More?"

I shrugged an apology. "It's just—I haven't eaten in four days."

Her hand leapt to her mouth. "Four days? Oh, you poor thing!" She ducked into the bushes and came back with a linen satchel, from which she took out a lump of cheese. She crept forward to drop it into my outstretched hand, then darted back. Ravenous, I gobbled it down, tearing hunks off with my teeth and swallowing them whole.

Phaith watched, wide-eyed. "Is that how boys eat?"

I looked up as I finished, suddenly embarrassed. "Uh, no. Okay, maybe some of us. I'm just hungry."

She handed me a wineskin. "Are you thirsty too? Here." Feeling her eyes on me, I drank it more carefully. She looked disappointed.

"Thanks," I said, putting the cork back in the goatskin. "I don't think I've ever been that hungry. Not even back in Troy."

"Troy?" she echoed.

"Where I came from. It's gone now. It was destroyed."

She nodded. "I've never been anywhere else. Just here." She gestured around us. "I'm a shepherdess."

"A shepherdess?" I asked, surprised. "There are sheep here too?"

She frowned. "No. Just cows. But I hate the word *cowherd*. It sounds so . . . ungraceful."

I wasn't sure what to say to that. "So you look after all the cows on the island?"

"That's right. Me and my sister." She frowned. "I don't want to talk about her. She's strange. Not like me."

Definitely no safe reply to that. Casting around for a change of topic, I smiled. "Thanks for the food, Phaith. I was hungry enough to eat a cow, horns to tail."

Her expression changed instantly. "Don't touch them!" she shouted, leaping to her feet, her eyes wild. "Don't you dare touch my cattle." She snatched a dagger from her belt and waved it at me. "Do you hear me? Not ever!"

Alarmed, I started to scramble to my feet but caught myself. "It's okay, Phaith," I said gently, sitting back down. "It's just a saying. Of course I wouldn't do *that*."

She stared at me for a moment longer. The fury faded slowly from her face and she squatted again and looked into my eyes. "I'm sorry, Alexi," she said, her expression anxious. "It's just that those cattle . . . well, I look after them for my father. They're protected. Bad things will happen if you hurt one." She shuddered, shaking her head. "Terrible things."

I stood up carefully. "I'd better be going. Thanks again for the food, Phaith."

She stepped forward and grabbed my shoulder as I turned

to go. "Really. *Don't.* And those men you're with, don't let them either."

I glanced back at her, surprised. "You know about them?"

A sly smile crept across her face. "Of course. I've been watching you."

CHAPTER THIRTEEN

The Cattle Are Lowing

URY WAS STANDING in the middle of camp. "This is what he won't let us eat, the men who took Troy! Lopex is afraid of cows!"

I had arrived back at the edge of camp as the late afternoon sun was stretching the shadows of inland hills across the beach. I was still unnerved by what Phaethusia had said, and the sight of Ury leading three milk-white cattle on leads into camp was twisting my stomach into a knot. What was he planning? I watched anxiously as he stopped near the cooking pit. The cows shambled to a halt behind him, chewing their cuds. The Greeks watched him from their driftwood seats and sand beds, their eyes as vacant as those of the cows.

"He listens to that witch and we starve. On an island full of cattle!" Ury paused for a moment to gather his strength. "He speaks of a curse on us, but we all heard that one-eyed monster. The curse is on him! Not us. Thanks to him, we've had more bad luck since we left Troy than we did in ten years before the gates. Lopex is the real curse!" he shouted.

The knot in my stomach tightened. Whatever it was that harming these cattle would trigger, Phaith had been too agitated even to talk about it.

Ury staggered for a moment, then stood upright again with a swig from his goatskin, splashing red wine across his tunic. "You know what he's doing? Waiting for us to die! Right now he's sitting somewhere eating roasted beef! Once we're dead he can sail home with all our treasure!"

Even for Ury, that sounded stupid. Lopex alone couldn't begin to push the ship off the beach, far less row it. I shook my head, my eyes on the knife that had appeared in Ury's hand. Kassander slipped silently up beside me from somewhere. "What is it? What's going on?" he murmured.

I was still on edge from my encounter with Phaith. "What does it look like?" I snapped.

In the centre of the camp, Ury was continuing to work himself up. "Look at you!" He took out his knife and waved it around at the men lying in the sand. "Heroes of Troy, starving because of an oath he forced on us!"

"Stupid," I muttered, thinking about Phaith's warning. "He's going to bring the curse down on us."

Beside me, Kassander shook his head. "Alexi, you must have realized by now that Ury is not the master of his fear."

I turned on him. "What the *korakas* do you know?"

He looked at me calmly. "I know enough not to get worked up over things I can't change. You might try it."

"What a surprise!" I muttered. "Kassander thinks we should do nothing!"

"How did you plan to stop him? We're slaves, Alexi. It's not in our power." Kassander pointed to Ury, now holding his knife. Long shadows from the hills had shaded Ury's face, but as he waved his knife over his head it flared red in the setting sun.

"Lopex will not defeat us!" he was shouting. "Can any death be worse than starvation?"

"He has a point, Alexi," said Kassander. "If we don't eat soon, we're going to die."

I grabbed his arm and stared into his face. "Didn't you hear what Lopex said? Those cattle are cursed!"

"Maybe so. But—" Kassander broke off and sniffed. "What's on your breath? Is that . . . cheese?"

I tried to back away but Kassander grabbed my arm. "Alexi, do you have food?" He bent toward my face, sniffing intently. "What have you been eating?" he demanded. "Have you been hoarding food?"

When I shook my head, he let go of my arm and stepped back, frowning. "I'm disappointed, Alexi," he said quietly. "Hiding food from starving men? Was that considered honest, back in Troy?"

Shame burned my cheeks. I hadn't even thought to bring any food back. As I opened my mouth to reply, a shout behind me made me turn. Ury's knife flashed down, plunging deep into the first cow's throat and spattering him with blood as the cow slumped to the ground with a strangled bellow. Shocked and anxious, I replied to Kassander more harshly than I'd meant to.

"Honesty? What would you know about it, *Arkadios*!"

His head jerked up and I realized how loud I'd been. We'd been speaking Anatolean, but his real name was distinctly Greek. It might have passed unnoticed, but I made the mistake of looking around to see if I'd been heard. A soldier watching Ury had glanced over at my voice.

"You!" he called. "What did you say? Get over here, both of you." *Kopros.* I started over reluctantly, then noticed that Kassander wasn't moving. I turned back toward him.

"Kassander! Didn't you hear?"

"Of course I did, boy," he said quietly, starting toward me. "But I couldn't move until you translated for me. They don't know I speak Greek, remember?"

Of course. He was staying in character as a Trojan slave. Well, to the Greeks, that conversation would look like a translation. He caught up with me and we approached, his head down and shoulders hunched like a frightened slave. The soldier was a squat, black-haired troll named Nikias. One of Ury's friends. Naturally.

"What did you call him, boy?" he said as we halted in front of him. He turned to his companion, frowning. "Arkadios?

Now why does that sound familiar?"

I stammered, trying to head off his train of thought. "Arkadios? No, I called him, um, *arachnios*. From his long arms and legs." Gods, a ten-year-old could do better.

Standing beside me, Kassander was saying nothing. "Translate for me, boy," he muttered. "I'm not supposed to understand, remember?"

"What? Oh—right. They think I've called you, well, you-know-what. Your real name."

Kassander turned his downcast head slightly to glance at me. "I know that, boy," he said quietly. "I'm Greek, remember? But we can still get out of this. Tell them I haven't done anything wrong. Sound like you're scared."

I wasn't sure what he was planning. "Sir?" I said to Nikias. "Please, he's just a slave. He didn't do it."

"Do what, boy?" he began, but Kassander threw himself to his knees, wrapping his arms around one of Nikias's stumpy legs.

"Please!" he whimpered. I froze. He'd spoken in Greek! But Kassander knew what he was doing. "Please," he said again in heavily-accented Greek, keeping his head down and shaking it so Nikias couldn't see his face. "Kassander good, please! No hurt!"

Nikias growled in disgust. "Get off me!" He said, trying to pull his leg free. "I said, get off me, you dirty Trojan coward. By Hermes, it's no wonder we took Troy. Get off!" He hooked Kassander under the chin with a sandaled toe and with a powerful snap of one thick leg sent him tumbling backwards. The thrust lifted Kassander half to his feet and he staggered back across the sand.

"Kassander!" I called. "Look out!" Off balance and staggering, Kassander stumbled backward straight into Ury, bent over as he skinned the first cow. They tumbled down together on the half-skinned, bloody carcass.

"What are you doing, you stupid *sueromenos*! I nearly cut my hand off!" Ury began, but stopped. Landing on their sides, they were facing one another, their noses almost touching. Kassander swung an arm up to hide his face but Ury caught his elbow.

"Wait!" he said, frowning. He forced Kassander's arm down and peered into his face. His eyes widened in shock.

"You?" he gasped. Dropping Kassander's elbow he scrambled up off the bloody carcass. Kassander stood up slowly, his face expressionless.

Ury gestured, his eyes wild. "Grab him! Don't let him get away!" Two dark men scrambled to comply, binding Kassander tightly by his shoulders. Ury walked around him, his knife waving warily, then stopped and put the edge against Kassander's throat. An unpleasant smile warped his face. "It *is* you!" he breathed. "Arkadios! The *lawagetas*!"

Nikias had stumped up beside them. "That's what that slave called him," he said, pointing at me. "Arkadios."

"He did?" Ury's unpleasant smile broadened. "This just gets better and better. Bring him here too." I was dragged over to stand beside Kassander. Ury stood before us, swaying slightly, the front of his tunic soaked in the heifer's blood. He reached for his goatskin and took another swig of wine.

"So the stories were true. You went over to the Trojans. I didn't believe them. Not Arkadios. *Respectable* Arkadios." He folded his arms across his chest and stood there for a moment, staring at Kassander.

"Bad move, traitor." He leaned forward, his face almost touching Kassander's. "But I've got you now." He stepped back and looked at me, his eyes narrow. "You too, slave. Hiding a traitor. Nobody will stop me if I kill you now."

Nikias had taken out his own knife, a wickedly curved dagger with a short blade. "So who gets it first?" he asked impatiently. "The traitor?" He pointed his knife at Kassander. "Or the slave?" The knife swung toward me.

A crafty look stole across Ury's face. "No." He beckoned to some men nearby. "Tie them up. Killing takes a full belly to enjoy properly."

Four of Ury's men hauled us up the beach to the *Pelagios*, Ury and Nikias following us. We were thrown to the ground, our hands and feet threaded through the bow boarding net and bound together with rawhide cord. As Nikias wrenched my tunic off my shoulders, Melantha's knife tumbled out beside me. I tried to slide over it but Ury pounced.

"What's this?" he said, snatching it up. "Who'd you steal this from?"

Nikias gave me a vicious kick in the side. "Answer your master, slave," he grunted.

"Didn't . . . steal it," I gasped, curling up around the pain. "Mine. Look at it—not Greek."

Ury looked at the pattern on the handle and his eyes narrowed. "You lying Trojan. This is a girl's knife."

"My . . . sister's," I said, wheezing. "A coming-of-age gift."

Nikias spoke from behind me. "I've seen that knife before." He stepped over my head for a better look in the dusk. "That's Sophro's," he added. "A trophy, he said."

"Sophronios?" Ury gave me another painful kick in the side. "How did you get his knife, you sack of *kopros*? You know what happens to slaves who steal?"

Gasping for breath, I couldn't speak. "Sophro told me he took it off a girl," Nikias said. "The night we took Troy."

Ury stopped short. "A girl?"

Nikias shrugged. "Some Trojan *kuna*. Found her lying against a well."

Kopros. This was exactly where I had hoped Ury's thoughts would never go. "Near a well," he said slowly. "A well?" His face contorted in thought.

Kassander's dry voice came from nearby. "You never change, do you, Ury? Kicking an unarmed slave—if someone ties him up for you first."

Ury spun around to face Kassander. "Shut up!" he roared. Dropping his wineskin, he leapt to smash Kassander's face with a fist, forgetting me entirely. The sound of furious, crunching blows came from Kassander's direction as Ury unleashed his rage. Sickened, I huddled with my head down, unable to watch.

Finally, his rage spent, he stopped and sniffed the air, now filled with the maddening scent of roasting beef. "Enjoy the smell," he said unsteadily. "I'll be back." He stumped back to the fire, where his men had slaughtered the other two cattle and begun skewering and grilling slices of beef.

There was no sound from beside me. My face burning like an open forge, I forced my head to turn.

"Kassander?"

Slumped against his bonds, he didn't answer.

"Kassander?" I took a breath. "I just want to say—I'm so sorry. You've always given me good advice. You lied about yourself, but you had good reasons. I wish I had kept my mouth shut."

Kassander heaved his head part way up to look over at me. Blood was trickling from both nostrils and his smashed lower lip. The skin around his left eye was turning black, while his right eye was already swelling shut. He began to shake his head but winced and stopped.

"I expected—" he broke off, coughing, and spat out a tooth with a mouthful of blood. "I expected to be caught long ago. You stopped that."

He paused for a rasping breath that made him wince again. "You translated. They never had to speak to me." He breathed heavily for a moment. "They would have known me . . . earlier, if they had." His head dipped again.

"Kassander!" I called. He didn't answer. "Arkadios! Listen to me!" He lifted his head slightly.

"We can still get away. They'll be busy for a while. Look at them." I nodded toward the centre of camp, where the Greeks were wolfing down half-raw skewers of beef the moment they came off the fire.

He shook his head, then winced. "How would we . . . get free?" he asked, his voice nearly inaudible. "And we'd need a distraction. A big one. Give us time to . . . escape."

A voice boomed out across the camp, rising easily above the crackling cooking fire and the noises from the Greeks. *"What in the name of the twelve immortals is going on here?"*

Lopex had returned.

A bulging sailcloth sack over one shoulder, he strode into the centre of camp where several Greeks were roasting beef over a fire and smashed the skewers from their hands. "Is this how men of Achaea respect their oaths?" he shouted, staring around at them as they froze in mid-mouthful. "Is this how you show your devotion? Breaking your word to the gods the moment you get hungry?"

He was some distance away from us but in the sudden silence every word rang clear. Dropping his sack, he turned to Ury and smashed him back-handed across the mouth, sending him staggering and knocking his skewer to the ground. "And you, Ury? Where is your honour? You who in my absence hold command, this is how you abuse it? You shame yourself. You shame us all, before the gods."

Ury half-straightened, his forearm raised to shield his face. Around them, the other Greeks watched silently to see what he would do. Ury glanced around and straightened slowly. "It's not my fault!" he burst out. "You left us here to starve! You wanted us to die!"

Lopex stared at him as though at a loss for words. Taking heart from his silence, Ury snatched up a skewer of raw beef from the slaughterboard by the fire—and bit off a mouthful. He held the skewer over his head and turned to face the camp. "We've eaten, and nothing has happened! If there's a curse on this meat, then curse me now!" He turned back to face Lopex once again and took another bite.

Lopex's sword hand crept out from his body, fingers flexing, and Ury took an uncertain step back. But Lopex's hand stayed where it was, and after a moment he sighed and shook his head. "You're a fool, Ury. I knew it was a mistake to give you authority, but until now I hadn't understood just how big a fool you were."

He lifted up the sack he had brought back into camp and faced the men. "At the southernmost end of this island is a rush marsh. I have spent three days identifying which plants are safe, and have returned with enough for several days' meals." He glanced expressionlessly at Ury. "But we are undone by your foolishness. Eat, then, if you have no respect for your oaths. But for any among you who have not already despoiled your honour before the gods, these shoots are the meal they intended for us."

He dropped the sack on the sand, pulled out a finger length of pale-green plant stalk and bit into it. "Pray hard for the winds to release us tomorrow. The curse is real, and you have unleashed it. Perhaps we can yet escape before it strikes."

He turned and caught sight of us, tied to the boarding nets of the Pelagios. "Ury!" he barked. "Why is my slave tied up? And why is our healer tied up beside him?"

Ury smirked. "Your slave, Lopex? You should have looked more closely. He's no more Trojan than you are. This is Arkadios the traitor! The man who went over to the Trojans!"

Lopex came across the beach to us and knelt to peer into Kassander's eyes.

"You haven't left much of his face for me to tell, Ury," he said mildly, "but yes, this is Arkadios." He glanced at me, lashed to the boarding net nearby. "And our Trojan healer?" he asked drily. "Is he a Greek turncoat too?"

"Well, no," Ury began, sounding less certain. "But he kept the traitor's secret." He frowned. "And there's something else . . ." His voice trailed off for a moment as he tried to remember, but Kassander's interruption earlier had snapped his strand of thought. "I'm sure he knew about Arkadios, at least," he added. "He called the traitor by his real name. I'll kill them both after we've eaten."

Lopex looked at him. "Has it occurred to you that knowing a man's name doesn't mean knowing his history? Or that most men would have done the same in his position?"

He turned back and pointed to Kassander. "Whoever he is, he is still my slave. I choose to leave him alive, for now. As for the boy, who were you planning for our new healer? Release him immediately."

Ury came over to cut my bonds, glaring at Lopex's retreating back. "I'll get you yet, boy," he muttered, sawing savagely at the cords on my wrists. "He may be blind but I'm not. I'll have your tongue in my collection soon enough." He shook his leather pouch at me.

My wrists and ankles had been bound so tight they had gone white, and it was some time before I could put any weight on my feet. When at last I could, I stood up and hobbled carefully over to Kassander, still bound. I looked at the knot binding his wrists but he shook his head. "Don't help me. Ury would love to catch you. Get back to camp."

He was right. Even treating Kassander's wounds would be all the excuse Ury needed. Feeling helpless, I hobbled toward the rear edge of the camp where the beach grass began, keeping clear of Ury while I worked the cramps out of my wrists and ankles. As a result, I was the first to see the curse begin.

Ury had ordered some men to carry the offal from the slaughtered cattle out of camp. The men had dumped it all— heart, lungs and other organs—in a sprawling pile in the long grass. As I limped back and forth, trying to walk some life back into my feet, I heard a strange noise from the pile, like an old man wheezing. I crept over and peered down into the grass.

At my feet, the offal was moving.

For a moment I thought there was an animal burrowing in it and stepped closer to look. The sound was coming from the pink, fleshy lungs themselves, expanding and contracting. Regular, bubbling gasps as the air rushed in and out. I stared in astonishment for a moment until something else caught my attention. Off to my left, one of the deep red cow hearts was pulsing too. Separated from its body, it was starting to beat rhythmically as if still alive.

I backed away, staring. Now one of the intestines started to move, coiling and pulsing like a giant, fleshy snake. A disembodied tail flicked at a phantom fly, and I lost my composure completely. Stumbling and scrambling, I backed away until I could turn around and run back into camp. Some of the Greeks looked up as I burst in among them, pointing back toward the offal dump, trying to form words.

"What's the matter, city boy? Never seen cow guts before?" Someone guffawed but suddenly stopped. Stretched out on the wooden slaughterboards near the main campfire, the jaws of the three carcasses had started to move in unison, a slow, rhythmic chewing as though they were working their cud in a field.

The two men nearest them scrambled up in alarm. Ury, his back to them as he chewed hunks off a skewer of beef, turned toward them. "What's your problem? Sand up your *gloutos*?" The men shook their heads, pointing. Ury looked over and leapt to his feet, dropping his skewer of beef. "Sweet mother of Zeus! What in the name of Ares *koprophage* is that!"

The men around me were scrambling to their feet, groping for their knives. From the cutting boards, a low noise began that grew louder until I recognized it as a pain-filled bellow. The skinless carcasses, the first little more than a skeleton, had lifted their heads and begun an agonized lowing, a sound that grew more insistent until it seemed to vibrate in my own teeth and throat. Around me, the Greeks clung to one another in fear as the curse unfolded.

First one flayed carcass, then the other two, lurched to their feet and hobbled off their planks onto the sand. Shedding shreds of flesh and muscle, they began to stagger among the terror-stricken men. Near the edge of camp, I huddled anxiously behind a bulky warrior, too frightened to move. How could this be happening? The three carcasses were staggering around blindly, their heads lifted as they howled their unearthly pain into the dusk.

The lead cow staggered toward me, ragged strips of flesh still trailing from its bloody bones. The soldier and I bolted in opposite directions through the panic-stricken mass of men. I found myself running toward the far side of the camp where the *Pelagios* was beached.

"Alexi! Stay here. It's safer."

For whatever reason, I had bolted toward Kassander, still bound hand and foot to the boarding net. Reassured by his tone, I slowed to a stop. His right eye was now swollen completely shut but the other searched my face, then flickered toward the chaos in camp. "I'm not sure . . . how you managed it, Alexi, but . . . nice distraction."

I turned back toward camp to watch the men, still darting in all directions. A few had swords out, but nobody was getting close enough to use them. Besides, if cutting their throats and pulling out the cattle's guts hadn't killed them, I couldn't see a sword doing much. Speaking of swords, I automatically felt for my knife but it wasn't there, of course. I reached through the net and started trying to unpick Kassander's wrist cords in the gloom. He nodded.

Suddenly there was a new noise. One of the soldiers had bent double and thrown up his half-chewed meal. He lifted his head and shrieked in terror. "Merciful gods! They're still alive . . . inside us!"

In the firelight, I could just make out some misshapen lumps in the puddle he had left behind. The hair on my arms rose. Were they moving? Shocked, I stared at Kassander but he seemed unfazed. "Just as well we didn't . . . eat any," he wheezed. He saw my expression and shrugged. "Panic never helps. Your master Lopex knows that better than any man I've ever met."

I glanced over through the gloom at Lopex's tent. In the near-darkness I could just make out his pale shape sitting on a camp stool, arms folded, watching his men flee the stumbling creatures. One by one the men stopped running and violently retched up their dinner.

A few of his men were pleading with him, but Lopex continued to watch in silence. Eventually he unfolded his arms and stood up. "Men of Ithaca!" he shouted, his tone demanding attention. "I warned you of the curse. Do you believe now?"

Despite their terror, many of the men stopped. Those who didn't were tripped and pinned by the others. Lopex waited.

Finally, when the only sound was that unearthly lowing, Lopex spoke. "If you want to live, listen now. You have seen what disobedience brings. From this point on I demand unquestioning obedience as the price of my help. *Do I have it?*"

An anxious affirmative quavered back from the men. Lopex looked around, unconvinced. "*I said, do I have it?*" he roared.

The men found the energy to roar back. "Yes!"

Lopex looked slowly around the camp at the terrified men. After what could have been a lifetime, he nodded. "Very well. Do *exactly* what I say. Polites, take five men to collect driftwood. Adelphos, take three more and chop the driftwood down to fire size, then bank the fire up. Ury, take ten men and rope those creatures. Three of you hold each one steady while the rest cut them into pieces no larger than your thumb. Everyone else, collect every single piece of each carcass— every hoof, hide, horn, scrap of offal, bone or flesh. Every piece of those creatures must be burnt away to ash. We may not be able to reverse the curse, but if we destroy all the signs, we may yet escape it. And tomorrow, wind or no wind, we will leave this island if we have to swim." The men scrambled to obey.

I nodded in admiration. Back on the island of the Cyclops, I'd seen him do the same thing, binding a mob of frightened men into a dedicated group with a few words.

The rawhide knot binding Kassander's wrists and ankles suddenly came free, and as I unlaced the remaining cord on his ankles, he pulled his hands from the net and clutched at my arm. "I've got to go, before anyone looks this way. When I'm gone, get away from this spot. Wipe away your tracks. Sleep on the far side of camp tonight. Near the Greeks. I won't see you again."

I nodded. "Kassander, I—"

He tugged his hands and feet out of the boarding net and got carefully to his feet, feeling his ribs and wincing. "You've helped me escape. All debts are paid now." He looked toward the camp. "A lot of debts were repaid tonight." He hobbled around the bow of the *Pelagios* and vanished into the night.

CHAPTER FOURTEEN

Revelation

A FURIOUS BELLOW WOKE me the next morning. Ury, of course. He was so angry he was hardly making sense, but I was pretty sure I knew what it was about.

"That *kopros*-eating traitor! Where is he!" he was roaring. I fought my way awake and rolled over to watch. Ury was stomping across the beach, kicking men awake as he passed as if he expected to find Kassander hidden in a Greek bedroll somewhere.

We had been up most of the night. Desperately relieved to have Lopex back in charge, the Greeks had jumped to follow his orders, incinerating the hacked-up remains of the cattle:

hides, bones, offal and all. I had been forced to clean up the puddles of vomit around the camp, scooping them up with a shovel and burning them away to ash in a sizzling bronze pan set up at one side of the huge fire. A disgusting job, but still better than what Pharos and Adelphos had been tasked with, loading the still-pulsing lungs and hearts onto a shield to carry to the pyre. Even cutting them into small pieces hadn't worked, and several men were kept busy sweeping the burning chunks of organ, flesh and bone back into the fire as they struggled to crawl away.

Dumping fresh meat directly onto the fire kept threatening to put it out, and two other soldiers were kept busy searching the nearby coast in the ship's *skaphis* for more driftwood, clutching torches against the moonless dark. The night was almost over by the time Lopex stirred the embers with his sword and declared the carcasses destroyed. "Now get some sleep, all of you," he added. "Tomorrow we leave. Unless any of you think you know better, of course." Ury stared at his feet as Lopex's gaze swept over him.

Now, with the morning breeze blowing away the guilty stench of burnt flesh, Ury had found his bluster again. "The traitor's bonds were untied," he shouted, holding up the rawhide cords that I had unpicked last night. "Someone here helped him escape!" I ducked my head beneath my sailcloth sheet as his glance came my way.

A second voice rang across the camp. "Ury!" It was Lopex,

standing beside his tent. "I need all hands to break camp. You are to waste no time on the traitor. Furthermore, your behaviour in my absence has disgraced you as a commander. I will no longer permit you in a command position." Ury opened his mouth to argue but was silenced by Lopex's fierce glance. He subsided, muttering.

After a breakfast of the gritty, chewy shoots that Lopex had brought back, we were put to work breaking camp. "There must be no sign we were ever here," Lopex announced. "Every scrap, every piece of shaped wood, pottery or bronze must be stowed on board, all cooking pits dug into the sand and buried. You, boy," he called to me, "take this shovel and fill in the cess trench."

I came over to take the shovel from him, but he held his grip for a moment. I looked up. "You helped Arkadios escape," he said quietly. I was about to protest but he waved me to silence. "I expected you would. Why do you think I had you untied?"

He must have seen my confusion. "A commander can't always give orders, Alexi. Sometimes he has to work through others." He let go of the shovel. "Off you go, then." I headed for the cess trench, wondering. Had I heard an apology in his voice? I shook my head. I didn't like being used. But like it or not, he was good at it. I frowned, choking the thought off angrily.

The cess trench that the Greeks used as a toilet marked the southern edge of their beach camp. It had been extended a dozen times since we arrived, now winding back on itself like a gigantic dirt snake. Many of the Greeks hadn't been too careful about filling it in after using it, and I had to work my way along its whole smelly length. It was mindless work, and my thoughts wandered back to the girl I'd met. Phaethusia. I stopped. Was she watching right now? I glanced up toward the near edge of camp, suddenly embarrassed to be cleaning a cess trench, but couldn't see anyone. I sighed. Even with her doe-eyed timidity—or maybe because of it—I realized I'd been hoping to see her again. Well, it wasn't likely to happen now.

Someone grabbed my shoulder. I turned hopefully, but it was Palakis, a soldier I didn't know very well, a younger man with a short, black beard.

"Come quick," he said nervously. "He's sore hurt. Slipped over the gunwale, see? Landed hard on the ground. I think there's something wrong, inside. It's my mate, you follow?"

I followed him across the camp, threading our way between half-buried cooking pits and stacks of bedrolls waiting to be loaded. At the rear edge of camp, the Greeks were standing in a circle around what sounded like a fight, but Palakis didn't slow down. "Come on, come on," he urged me, tugging at my tunic. "He's sore hurt. Broke his leg, maybe."

"I thought you said there was something wrong inside?" I asked, confused.

"Yes, yes, that too," he replied. "But hurry along, he's poorly, I tell you."

He led me around the stern of the *Pelagios* to the starboard side, away from camp. I could make out someone lying in the shade of the hull and covered by a blanket. Only four over-loaded spar poles were propping the ship up on this side, and I came over cautiously to kneel beside the injured man. I had just time to wonder what the blanket was for when Palakis announced, a little too loudly, "He's here."

The man under the blanket rolled over and whipped it off. It was Ury. Before I could leap back, he had grabbed both my arms and thrown me to the ground.

This was no time for pride. "Help!" I shouted. "Pharos! Deklah!"

Ury smiled nastily as he straddled my chest, pinning my arms painfully under his knees. "They won't hear you, slave. I made a—" he hesitated, frowning, "a distraction." He sounded proud of himself. "Palakis, go join the fight. Keep it going."

My sister's knife appeared in his hand as Palakis left. "Recognize this, Trojan? Now, I got to thinking this morning. That girl by the well, she was your sister, you said. So if she was there where my brother died, where were you?" His eyes narrowed. "You were there too. It was you that Takis saw on the steps behind my brother. It was you that killed him."

I shook my head but Ury just smiled, a slow, nasty grin that split his face like a wound. "And I wanted to kill you just for being Trojan. I had no idea." He shook his head. "All this time, my brother's killer was right here." He leaned down close to my face and the knife tip caressed my neck. "Lopex isn't here to stop me now, boy. I can take my time." The knife point began to slide up my neck toward my left ear.

As I struggled to get free, I realized something. The familiar wave of fear, the sickening terror that stopped my thoughts— it wasn't coming. This time, what I was feeling was . . . anger. A cold, furious anger at Ury for terrorizing me for so long. And at myself for letting him do it.

Ury paused uncertainly as he saw my expression change. "Ury?" I whispered, quietly scraping up two handfuls of sand behind his back. "There's one thing you need to know. Something you're wrong about."

Ury frowned and leaned down to hear, as I knew he would. I drew a deep breath and shouted the truth into his face. "It was my sister! Ury, your brother was killed by a girl!" Shocked, he rocked backward and his knees came off my arms for an instant. I yanked them free and thrust my hands up to grind the sharp sand into his eyes. Bellowing like a wounded bull, he leapt up, clawing at his face. I scrambled to my feet and started to run off, but stopped as I passed a pile of unused spars. Running away would solve nothing. Was there another way? I glanced back, watching him curse as he rubbed his red and streaming eyes. I looked around. We were still alone, thanks to Ury. Perhaps this time I could teach him to fear me.

I picked up one of the unused spars from the pile and ran back with it. He had my sister's knife, but it would be no help against the longer range of a spar. Ury's puffy eyes widened as he saw me coming, and he grabbed for the spar beside him.

With so few spars propping up the ship up on this side, it was wedged tight, and he braced one foot against the base of the hull as he pushed with both hands. Already bent under its load, the spar snapped suddenly, leaving Ury sprawling on the sand.

Someone behind me scooped me up one-handed and hauled me away from the ship. I turned angrily to find Pharos, but a noise behind me drew my attention back. With one spar gone, the remaining three were even more overloaded. They creaked and bent further, and the ship began to tip over toward us. Ury was trying to scramble out of the way, but he seemed to be stuck. I peered closely into the shade of the hull and realized with shock that his foot was caught, pinned in the sand beneath the hull as it shifted.

He looked up and spotted us. "You! Slave boy!" he shouted anxiously. "Come here! Pull me out!"

For some people I would have risked it, but not Ury. I turned to Pharos, but he shook his head silently, pointing at the last three spars. They were bending like bows, and even as we watched, one snapped with a loud crack, sending pieces of wood flying. The ship heeled further.

"Pharos!" called Ury, his tone panicked. "Help me!"

I looked at the spar in my hand. Surely even Ury didn't deserve this. I was about to move forward to put it in place but Pharos grabbed my shoulder. "Too late," he murmured.

He was right. The last two spars, carrying a load far beyond them, snapped at the same instant. With a great crashing and clanking as the storage vessels and plunder shifted in the hold, the ship rolled slowly onto its side, crushing Ury's legs and torso into the sand. Only his head and one arm were still visible as the ship came to rest. He raised his head to look at me, trying to say something, but collapsed back into the sand.

Spotting the ship's movement, the other Greeks were pouring around it from both sides as Pharos and I stood together, facing the ship. "Ury's men started fight," he said. "Fight rang false to Pharos. Too much shouting, too little blood. And then Pharos could not see Ury or healer."

I nodded, overwhelmed by what I had just seen. Should I have tried to save him? Pharos spoke as though he could hear my thoughts. "Not worth saving. Ship needs healer."

Lopex strode up. "Boy? Alexi! What in Athene's name is going on here?"

I stammered, looking for an explanation, but Pharos spoke. "Pharos saw. Ury, foolishly pulling propping pole from flank of ship. Trapped beneath as ship rolled. Dead by own hand."

Lopex looked at the spar pole in my hand and I cursed silently. "Then what are you doing with that, boy?"

Pharos rode effortlessly to the rescue again. "Carrying to prop ship up again. Pharos held him back. Too dangerous. Needing healer more than foolish brute."

Lopex peered at us both in turn, but Pharos's expression gave nothing away. I struggled to keep my face still.

At last, Lopex nodded. "I always thought Ury would die in

a fight. Or with a knife in his back. I didn't see this." He paused thoughtfully. "Come on, then. We need to right the ship." He strode off.

I turned to Pharos, amazed. "Thanks. That was . . . quick."

He shrugged. "Pharos told only truth." A slight smile showed through his beard. "And if some truth unsaid, who is harmed? No one living."

I nodded. "Ury would have killed me." Pharos didn't react. Was he feeling guilty? "If anyone ever deserved to die, he did," I added. "He was an animal. Like his cousin."

Pharos's head twitched and I recalled that he was also a cousin of Ury's. "Not you!" I added. "Sophronios, I meant."

Pharos said nothing, waiting for me.

"He killed my sister, back in Troy. At least," I added, recalling Kassander's words, "he told me he did."

Pharos turned toward me. "Sophronios, with your sister?"

"He found her lying by the well and . . . cut her throat." I squeezed my eyes to keep the tears away.

Pharos shook his head. "Your sister that was, by well? In lower town of Troy?"

I nodded. "She killed his brother. But I was there."

Pharos looked puzzled. "There with Brillicos, on that night? You?"

"When the Greeks came—" I hesitated, uncertain.

Pharos nodded. "Tell story. Pharos does not mind."

After keeping it a secret for so long, it was a relief to let it out. "When you, the Greeks I mean, entered Troy, Ury's brother

Brillicos found Melantha in our room. She stabbed him in the neck as he carried her down the steps. But I was watching from the doorway."

"Ahh." Pharos breathed a long sigh of understanding. "Then you, Ury was seeking!"

I nodded. "Takis and Deklah saw someone on the steps and thought he did it. It was dark, so they never realized it was me. Ever since then, Ury has wanted to find the person on the steps."

Pharos frowned. "But cutting of throat, Sophronios said? Not he. Pharos, in same squad with Sophronios that night. Not permitting."

I looked up at him. "What do you mean?"

"A liar, was Sophronios, ever since boy. Never to believe. Listen now. Came our squad to square in lower town of Troy. Near steps, we saw a girl, lying dead against well. But pretending, she was. As Sophronios came, she sat up, slashed his nose with knife. Sophronios grabbed it, angry, ready to kill. Pharos stopped his hand. Not killing women, never."

I looked at him, not daring to understand. "Then what happened to her?"

Pharos shrugged. "Now? Only gods may know. But on that night, alive she was. Alive, running. Sophronios was for chasing her, but Pharos held him back. A woman like that, planning, slashing, escaping, is surely alive still."

I stared at him, feeling a great bubble of hope rising in my chest. Melantha—could it be true? Had Sophronios lied? I shook my head, trying to clear it, as a shout came from the ship.

"Men!" It was Lopex, standing on the port flank that was now the highest part of the ship. "The wind has died!" I looked over toward him and realized he was right. The onshore wind that had thwarted our every attempt to leave the island had dropped at last. "We must get to sea now, before it returns! Abandon the camp. I want every man to help right the *Pelagios* and push her off the beach immediately!"

Pharos and I hastened to help. Once the ship was righted and pushed into the water, two of Ury's swarthy minions were tasked with burying his crushed remains, battered into pulp by the ship's keel. They hadn't much heart for the task, or stomach either, and I watched out of curiosity as they scraped the remains of his carcass out of the sand and folded it to stack on a shield, then carried it over to dump into the end of the cess trench I'd left unfilled earlier.

I trailed behind the Greeks as we waded out to the ship and boarded. The wind that we all expected to blow us back didn't come, and we rowed out easily and caught a warm north breeze offshore. Behind us, only the outline of a couple of half-buried cooking pits gave any hint that men had lived there, and died.

I closed my eyes and leaned back on the rail. Melantha. Alive. Or had she died since? My drifting thoughts snagged on something: I hadn't seen her in Hades. I'd noticed it at the time but hadn't seen the significance. *We're drawn to the peo-*

ple we knew in life, Elpenor had said. And I hadn't seen her. I smiled to myself. Of course she'd escaped. She was a survivor. A fighter too, it seemed. Since Troy, I had let events blow me about like a dead leaf, while Melantha had been planning, thinking, getting away.

Getting away. That made all the difference. If she was alive, I could find her. If she was a slave, I would free her.

But first, I had to escape.

WORDS THAT MAY PUZZLE YOU

We don't know that much about the language of bronze-age Greece. In 1200 BCE, the time of the Trojan War, what we now think of as ancient Greece was still centuries in the future. Although Homer shows the Greeks and Trojans speaking to each other on the battlefield, the Trojans most likely spoke a different language. I've called it Anatolean, after the region, but nobody knows for sure. Throughout the book, I've used classical Greek words and expressions. Who knows? Perhaps the same expressions were also popular five hundred years before, during the Trojan War. Here is a list of the Greek words used, with their English translations:

Akonitos: Aconite. Poisonous root of plants in the monk's-hood family.

Amphora: A large urn with two handles for carrying and pouring liquids. Smaller than a *pithos*.

Arachnios: A nickname Alexi creates from the Greek *arachne*, which means spiderweb. It was also the girl in the famous story of the weaving contest, which Alexi would certainly have known.

Basternion: A litter, or ornate chair on a platform carried by slaves. Reserved for the rich and powerful.

Chiton: A man's tunic.

Eksepsis: Blood poisoning. The English word "sepsis" comes from the same root.

Gloutos: Buttocks.

Hagios: A Greek condition meaning, approximately, "protected by the gods." The best English equivalent might be "sanctified."

Himation: A garment, more like a cloak, probably worn overtop something like a *chiton*.

Houmos: Hummus, the middle-eastern garlic and chickpea dip. Probably not an authentic ancient Greek word.

Khalash: No meaning. Just something the Cicones said when they stabbed someone. An English translation might be "Yahoo!" or perhaps "Take that, you *kopros* sniffer!"

Koprolith: A fossilized or otherwise petrified piece of *kopros*. Source of the English word *coprolith*.

Kopros: Ahem. Dung.

Koprophage: Someone who eats *kopros*.

Koprophile: Someone who loves *kopros*.

Kottabos: A Greek drinking game that involved flicking drops of wine from their goblet at a target.

Kuna: A word with a variety of meanings, one of which is (only literally) a female dog.

Kylix: A wide-mouthed, shallow drinking goblet.

Krater: A large vessel for mixing water and wine. About the size of a punch bowl.

Lawagetas: A mid-level military commander.

Lotos: Untranslated. Homer refers to the "lotos-eaters," from which we get the modern spelling of "lotus eaters." He describes it as a "flowery fruit." The seed pod of the opium poppy, from which we get heroin, could be called that.

Methusai: Drunken women. An insult, especially when applied to men.

Nothos: A person of no legitimate family, or more specifically, of unknown father. An insult.

Ophion: Opium. Not clear that this word is authentic. Also means *serpent*.

Pelagios: The name—at least in this version—of Odysseus's ship.

Pestillos: Pestle, as in "mortar and—." Probably not authentic.

Pithos: A large urn with a wide mouth for transporting liquids and grains.

Rhyton: A cone-shaped cup or glass, often with a hole at the bottom from which you could pour wine or liquid directly into your mouth.

Sakcharis, Sakchar: Sugar. It's unlikely that the Greeks had the granulated white form that we're used to.

Skatophage: An eater of *skatos*.

Skatos: Also known as *kopros*.

Stratiotai: One of a wide range of words the Greeks had meaning soldier.

Suagroi: Wild pigs.

Sueios ekpneusis: Literally, bad smelling gas from a pig.

Sueromenoi: People with a romantic attachment to pigs. Singular would be *sueromenos*.

Troglos: Short form for the ancient Greek *troglodytos*, or cave dweller.

Xeneon: The guest room of a house. Since there were no hospitals, a doctor would examine or operate on you in his *xeneon*. Ancient Greeks didn't do many operations, but they did do amputations. The stumps were probably sealed and disinfected by cauterizing them with a burning torch. Chances of survival weren't that high.

Xenia, Xenios: The ancient Greek concept of the honour of hospitality. To the Greeks, giving gifts, especially amongst high-born families, was as much a source of honour as receiving them.

ABOUT THE AUTHOR

 Greek mythology has fascinated me ever since I discovered a copy of Bulfinch's *Mythology* in my father's library as a child. Even so, my writing career took a twenty-year detour through software development before I became a full-time writer. I began with Homer's *Odyssey* because it's a classic story, but one that nowadays is rarely read outside of university courses. I wanted to create a version that young people would read for fun: a realistic adventure, told not by the traditional heroes but by an outsider. For centuries, readers have been seeing the destruction of Troy through the eyes of the Greeks; I felt it was time to see it through the eyes of a Trojan. *Cursed by the Sea God* continues the adventures of Alexi the slave from the point that *Torn from Troy* leaves off. The third book of the trilogy is underway now in Toronto, where I live with my family, watching the winters grow steadily milder and the summers muggier. We have no dog—yet. For a preview of the concluding volume, or to contact me, please visit patrickbowman.ca.

DON'T MISS THE TRIUMPHANT
CONCLUSION TO THE
ODYSSEY OF A SLAVE TRILOGY

To find his sister, Alexi must
penetrate the fortresses of the
Greeks and escape alive,
encountering humans even more
terrifying than the monsters
of his past.

TO READ THE FIRST CHAPTER
OF THE CONCLUDING VOLUME, VISIT

patrickbowman.ca

MARQUIS

Québec, Canada

RECYCLED
Paper made from
recycled material
FSC® C103567
www.fsc.org

Printed on Enviro 100% post-consumer EcoLogo certified paper,
processed chlorine free and manufactured using biogas energy.

100%   PERMANENT   BIO GAS ENERGY